The Truth in Every Lie

The Truth in Every Lie

SMB

International Standard Book Number 13: 978-0-692-95474-4
10: 0-692-95474-0

Published by Ross and Fifth Press

First and for most I want to thank God for giving me the ability to write this novel and the understanding of being an author. Without you none of this would have been possible.

For my younger self, this is for you. For when you thought you weren't enough.

For my family and friends, thank you for believing in my dream and always supporting me. I love you.

For all of you reading, thank you for your support and patience. You are greatly appreciated.

Chapter 1

It was exactly 3:47 a.m. when I got the call about my baby brother Jean. My grandmother called me crying and screaming his name.

"Grandma? What's going on? What happened to Jean?"

"Baby, Jean has been killed, I woke up to gun shots and when I looked out of the window I saw a man lying …."

"Grandma I'm coming over."

I hung up the phone and ran downstairs to grab my keys off of the kitchen table. My husband, Blake, was sitting in the dining room eating a sandwich. He was sitting down in his usual chair by the balcony window. He was wearing his dark blue robe and black dad slippers. Blake was calm. I didn't notice him at first when I reached the kitchen; I thought he would have been locked away in his office, but he wasn't.

"Oh my God Blake, you scared the crap out of me. What are you doing up this late?"

"I could ask you the same thing? You know you are the one running out of here at 4 in the morning like someone has died."

"Yes someone did die; Jean was shot in front of my grandmother's house just a few hours ago, and I am on my way over there now. Do you want to come with me?"

"No baby, you know your grandma doesn't like me, and I know she is probably a mess right now. You go on, and I'll wait here for you to get back."

Blake all of a sudden got silent and looked out of the balcony window in the kitchen. He had this look on his face that I just couldn't read. I was so annoyed at the fact that he didn't want to come with me since he is my husband, and he was Jeans best friend. I looked over at him and he was still calm as ever.

2

"Are you fucking kidding me Blake, my brother just was shot and you don't want to come with me to see what's up? What the fuck man? Yo, I swear to God …."

Blake jumped up and grabbed my arm.

"You swear to God what Janelle? What?"

"Get off of me right now."

As I snatched my arm back, I stormed out of the house crying while I jumped into the SUV Blake had bought me last Christmas. I couldn't stop thinking about how he didn't even try to comfort me at such a serious time as this. My brother and Blake were friends since high school. They had only fell off a little while ago over something that they both wouldn't tell me about. I was extremely uncomfortable going over to my grandmother's because I wasn't sure how I was going to react if my brother's body was still lying on the ground or if the blood on the yard would destroy me.

As I drove over there, all I could do was think about my brother. I could never forget about that time he and I were in school at the pep rally, and this girl wanted to fight me. I didn't want to fight her because someone had spread a rumor that I had had sex with her man the week before. Her entire plan was to jump me with a few of her other friends. That night she had come up to me. We began arguing, and then all of a sudden she punched me. The last thing I remember was her friend dragging her off of me, and Jean was fighting her boyfriend. That night meant the world to me because Jean and I usually never had issues at school. I was the quiet one, and Jean was popular. I was so happy seeing my brother fight for me. He was defending me. Ever since then, Jean and I were a lot closer. We never went out to parties and school events without each other. We had each other's back since then. And now to have to see my brother's dead body or to see my grandparent's faces right now was going to destroy me. I didn't expect this to ever happen to Jean because he was well liked. He didn't have problems with anyone. So for someone to murder my brother was so confusing.

By the time I got to my grandmother's house, there were tons of people still outside. I jumped out of the truck and looked to my

4

right to see my brother's body on the front lawn just lying there lifeless. I ran over to his cold, dead body. He was lying there helpless; he seemed like he'd died in pain. His face was not peaceful. Jean's face was not of someone who died. His face read, "I was murdered, and I suffered."

I picked Jean up and held him in my arms. Jean's body was cold and motionless. As I sat on the lawn behind the yellow tape, I could hear my grandmother screaming in the background. My grandpa was trying to quiet her down. She just kept on screaming. This police officer came over to me. At first, he had just stood there staring at me. I knew he wanted me to let my brother go and move away from the crime scene but I couldn't. I couldn't leave him there on the ground. His body was covered in blood. The ground underneath him was also covered in his blood. My brother was no longer warm. He was dead. The officer then leaned down and touched my shoulder. His hands were warm, and I immediately started crying. I was crying so hard that I could no longer keep my brother in my arms. I laid his head down softly on our lawn and got up from the spot. When I stood up, the police officer helped me walk over to the porch. He made sure I got inside, and he then made me sit on the sofa in the den. My grandmother was walking up behind us, and she sat down next to me. I sat there lifeless; I couldn't believe that I was just holding my brother's dead body and didn't even get to say goodbye. I didn't get to speak to my brother today or even the last three days. He was on vacation with his girlfriend, and they had just gotten back this morning. It wasn't right for him to leave the earth the way that he did. I couldn't understand who would do this to him. I needed to know who and why they did this.

I watched a bunch of police officers come in and out of the house asking my grandparents questions. About seven different men were walking in and out whispering to each other, trying not to let us know if they found any evidence. There was a guy who stayed inside watching us. I didn't know why he was there because it's not like we were hiding anything. No one there was ever capable of murder. I knew for a fact that Jean's girlfriend wasn't either because she was pregnant with their daughter. She was eight months pregnant, and she loved my brother. Jean was going to marry her and everything.

He had his whole life planned out with her. He knew what he was

going to do with his life; he didn't ever fall short. I don't know what

the person was pissed about, but whoever it was didn't want my

brother to succeed in life. They could've taken his life weeks ago or

even months ago. This person really wanted to hurt Jean and his

family, which he had succeeded. I was hopeless; I wanted to find out

who had murdered my brother. I got up from the sofa and walked

over to the officer that was sitting down at the dining room table

watching us. He looked to be about in his late fifty's. He had short

gray hair and a gray mustache. This officer had to be about two

hundred and sixty pounds. If this weren't such a bad time, I would

whisper to my grandmother about his weight. My grandmother

always used this saying when it came to people that weighed a lot.

She would always say, "Peace be with them because we all know

that the jeans they have on are no longer in peace. They are in hell."

She always made jokes about everything. My grandmother was

7

always in a good mood. We never caught her upset or angry; she hid that from us really well.

The police officer stood up from the old wooden chair my grandfather refused to throw away, and he reached out and extended his arm. He motioned for a handshake. After about twenty seconds, the officer finally spoke.

"I am so sorry for your loss. Can I get you anything?"

"Thank you, but what I need right now are answers."

"My guys are working hard to find out who is responsible. You need to know that this won't be solved overnight. It may take a few weeks to months before we catch the guy and that's if we do. Murders aren't easy cases; they require a lot of work."

"Can I ask you a question?'' I asked the officer with concern.

"Yes sure," he replied.

"How many cases do you guys solve when murder is involved?"

"To be honest with you, not many. We usually have a lot of evidence but always seem to be missing one thing."

"So basically what you are telling me is that you will never find out who killed my brother and justice will never be served."

"No ma'am that's not what I am saying. What I am saying is that we do not always find out who the killer is but there are some cases where we do. It just takes time."

"I don't have time! We don't have time!" I walked away from the officer before he could say another word. I had to walk away before he had said anything else stupid. He wasn't making any sense; he just kept repeating himself. I don't know why he was there; he was not prepared to talk to families of the victims. He needed a new job.

When I was walking back to where my grandparents were sitting, there was a woman talking to them. I couldn't figure out who she was because I could only see the back of her head, but something about her was familiar. I just couldn't put my finger on it.

I walked over to where they were talking. I stood there for a few seconds, and then my grandfather stopped her from talking and introduced us. She was some lady from the church who I'd never met, but she said she'd heard a lot about me, and she knew Jean very well. She was talking so much that I didn't even notice that the police were gone and the ambulances were pulling off the street. Outside of the house, people were still standing around talking. From where I was, I could see no one moving. I walked behind the sofa that was in front of the living room windows and closed the blinds.

"Janelle honey, please come and sit down." My grandfather always called me by my name; he never called me Nelly like everyone else. When I walked over to where they were sitting, the lady from their church smiled at me and left the living room. My grandmother got up and walked her to the front door. My grandmother looked like she was having a hard time walking. She seemed to be very weak.

"Janelle, I need you to call Christine for me and tell her what happened to Jean. I cannot do it. Can you do that for me?"

"Yes, grandpa I can do that. Can I ask you something?" I sat up straight and fixed the blue shirt that I had on.

"Grandpa, do you have any idea of who could have done this?"

"No, I have no idea, I was trying to figure out who. But Jean didn't have any enemy's, so I don't understand who would want him dead."

"I don't know Grandpa, but I'm going to go home, I can't stay. I will call you guys tomorrow."

"Okay Janelle, I love you. Call me or text me when you get to the house."

"Okay, love you too." As I walked to my car, my grandmother was outside on the porch sitting in the rocking chair that Jean built for her birthday last year. She looked heartbroken. I've never seen her look like that; it was actually painful. I walked

11

over to her, and she was just staring at the ground. My grandmother usually is never lost for words, but today she was. I couldn't quite read her emotions. I knew she was upset, but I wasn't sure how much. I didn't want to leave my grandmother at the house, but I knew my grandfather would take good care of her and right now I needed Blake to hold me. I needed to get into bed and sleep.

Walking to my car, I noticed someone was standing down the street staring in my direction. I wasn't sure if I knew this person, but something about them looked familiar. The person stood there not moving; they were wearing dark colors so I couldn't recognize them at all. They were also standing in front of a car that looked familiar, but I wasn't too sure if I knew whose car that was or if it was just some nosey neighbor. Finally, I got into my car and noticed that I had ten missed calls and text messages from Blake.

When I left home, I was so pissed off at Blake, but all I wanted to do was lie with him. I wanted him to run me a bath and pour me a glass of wine. I wanted to listen to music and let my body drown in the hot bath water. My body was sore, and my head was

12

killing me. I really needed to relax. My brother had died, and my grandparents were going to be hurting again. I wasn't ready for that and what made it worse is that my parents weren't there to make everything right. My mother and father were such great people. If it weren't for that plane crash, they would have still been there with us, but I was glad they were gone because I didn't want to see my parents mourn their dead son.

I made it home, and Blake was lying down in the bed sleeping. I walked over to the bed and sat down; he must've been awake still because he got up and grabbed me by my arm and pulled me in for a kiss. When we kissed, it felt different. It felt like he was hiding something. It just didn't feel right, but I played it off like everything was okay because I already had enough on my plate. I got up from the bed and went into the bathroom to take a shower when I noticed that I did not have on my wedding ring. I always have my ring on. As I walked into the bedroom, I looked on the nightstand and saw it sitting there on top of one of Blake's books. I went back into the bathroom and took a hot shower. All I could think

13

about was Jean and who would have wanted to take him out like that. Jean was such a great guy. I mean, of course, we all have our flaws and issues but not Jean. He was one of the sweetest guys left in our neighborhood. He had two jobs and was about to have a kid with his high school sweetheart. Jean had the rest of his life ahead of him and for someone to take his life like that has got to be Satan.

After my shower, I went into the bedroom. Blake was no longer in bed. I took my time putting on my silk pajamas that were lying on the bed. Blake always knew just what I needed whenever I was stressed or upset about something. I love that about him. I don't know if that kiss meant anything, but he was defiantly showing me love and wasn't going to act like I wasn't mourning my dead brother. I don't know how Blake wasn't upset about Jean's death since they were best friends back in high school. If they were still friends, I probably wouldn't know how to handle dealing with Blake because I still remember the day his mother died; he was heartbroken. My brother and I had to literally pull Blake from the

14

bed after about four or five weeks; he would hardly eat or drink anything. That was the first time I had ever seen Blake depressed. He never really showed his emotions when it came to personal things, but that day he didn't care. That day he showed me his heart. If I didn't think I knew him before that, I definitely knew then.

The next day Blake and I woke up together with the television and the lights on in the bedroom. I didn't even remember going to sleep because we were both up talking about Jean, and I spent most of the night crying. Blake held me all night and made sure that I had extra tissues by the bed. He cooked me dinner and didn't ask me if I was okay when he knew that I wasn't. I wondered when Blake would mourn the death of my brother since they used to be best friends back before they fell out. I didn't see Blake cry; he didn't even act like he had lost a friend, and he didn't even look like it had affected him. It was like Jean was just a family member I was close with and someone that Blake had only met that one time at my family reunion. Blake was the one person I expected, besides my grandparents, to be upset over his death, but he wasn't. Blake didn't show any grief. It was weird, and I wasn't buying any of it. Maybe he was waiting for the funeral. I hadn't had time to go by my grandparents' house to help with the funeral arrangements. I didn't want to go over there and be reminded of where my dead brother's body had been lying cold and lifeless. That will always stick with me, and it was way too soon to go back there. I knew my granddad would be calling me soon. My grandparents wouldn't be able to pay for everything, so I knew they would call eventually. I knew that I would have to go home, but I just couldn't get myself to get out of the bed and make that trip. I didn't want to be reminded of his death; I didn't want to remember that day at all.

Chapter 2

After laying in the bed for two hours listening to Blake snore and thinking about Jean, I got up and went into my closet. I reached up and pulled the black wire that was hanging from the ceiling, which lead to the little crawl space in our attic. The door made a loud creek, and I thought I had awakened Blake, but I didn't. He was still sleeping; he didn't move a muscle. I climbed the short ladder, which was five steps and crawled on the hardwood floor that Blake had installed. The only thing that was up there were the keepsakes of Jean and I, the both of my parents, things from our wedding, and a few things I kept from high school. Immediately, I saw the box that said family on it. It was covered in dust and was taped closed. I ripped the tape off the top of the cardboard box, and the first thing that caught my eye was a family picture of my mother and father holding Jean and I on their laps. My parents didn't die until we both were older. Jean and I were both in Middle school when they passed away. On the day of my parent's funeral, my father's parents had not shown up. They were not speaking to him. The only person who showed up was my dad's half-sister, Ann. Jean and I never met our other grandparents because they didn't like my mother. My dad would tell us stories about them and how they hated my mother. He didn't like that they hated her so much; he didn't speak to them since he had married her and went against everything they believed and thought was right for him.

I went into the rest of the box looking at the remainder of the pictures that I had with my parents. We all looked so happy together in each one. I sure did miss my parents; I didn't get to have a lot of time with them when I was a child because my father was in the military and my mother worked a lot. Jean and I spent a lot of time with our grandparents and each other. I don't resent my parents for not spending time with us, but I do hate that they had died in a plane crash.

As I was looking through the box of keepsakes, I could hear Blake in the bedroom. It sounded like he was opening and closing the drawers on our dresser. He didn't say a word; he just kept going

through the drawers. I closed the box and headed back down the

steps to the closet, and Blake was now sitting on the bed. He was

staring at his phone; he didn't even look up to see me standing in the

closet doorway. I walked over to the bed and lay down next to him. I

glanced over at his phone. He was emailing someone. I couldn't

really see who or what exactly he was typing, but what I could see

was that he mentioned a name of some sort of pills. I didn't know if

Blake was addicted to pills because we both weren't on any

medications. We didn't keep pills in our home unless they were

antibiotics from when we are sick, so I wasn't sure if he was

emailing someone for him or about work. After Blake had finished

typing the email, he got up and went downstairs. He acted as if he

didn't even see me; he didn't even look at me. I didn't understand

what was going on with him because just last night we were fine, we

were talking, loving each other. Then, all of a sudden, he was not

speaking or looking at me. I got up from the bed and decided to call

my grandparents to see if they needed anything from me and what they were planning on doing about Jean's funeral arrangements. My grandparents shouldn't have needed to plan the death of their grandchild; it wasn't right. Jean and I should have been planning funeral arrangements for them. I always thought they would die or be in their nineties if they had ever had to go to one of our funerals, but no my grandparents were young and had to suffer. They had to live the rest of their lives with the image of my brother's dead body on their front lawn.

The phone rang three times before my grandfather picked up. I could hear other people in the background. The doorbell lightly rang, and I could hear my grandmother saying that she will go and get it. I could only imagine who was over the house. My grandfather took a deep breath into the phone before he said hello.

"It's me, Janelle, Grandpa."

"Yes, I know Janelle, are you coming over later?"'

"Yes, I'll come over, do you guys want me to come over now?"

"Yes, please come over now, we need to talk about the funeral arrangements with you."

"Okay, I will be over in an hour."

"We will be here, oh and bring Blake with you. He should be here."

"Okay, we will be there soon. I love you."

"I love you too."

After we said I love you, all I heard was the dial tone. My grandpa would usually have more to say; we sometimes talked for hours, and then my grandma would pick up the other house phone and join the conversation. We did that almost twice a week.

I hung the phone up and grabbed a pair of light blue jeans out of my closet. I was looking for my Bob Marley graphic t-shirt that is usually hanging in the closet by the door. It wasn't there, and I know I didn't wear it at all. I had just bought it a few months ago. Jean and I were in the mall together one Tuesday night, and we came across a stand that was selling t-shirts dirt cheap, and there were only two

Bob Marley shirts left on the stand, so we thought why not and

bought them. Jean had died in his last night. His entire shirt was

covered in blood. I couldn't find mine. I thought I hadn't worn it

until I saw it on the top of the dirty clothes hamper. It was strange

seeing it there because I could have sworn I didn't wear it, but I

guess I did. I walked out of my closet and grabbed one of Blakes

favorite work shirts. I took the white one with the black collar off of

the hook and put it on. Blake had an obsession for all types of button

up shirts. Sometimes I would find pajama button ups in his drawer

with the tags still on them, he doesn't wear them to bed but collects

the ones that he likes. It's really strange but that was his thing. Every

year during Thanksgiving and Christmas, he would buy the most

button up shirts since they would be on sale.

I went downstairs into the living room, and I could smell

bacon cooking. Blake loved to cook; that's all he had ever done. I

cook very little. It's not that I can't cook, but Blake's love for

cooking always got in the way, so I didn't need too. When I walked

into the kitchen, Blake had an empty egg carton filled with shells on the counter. There was a piece of bacon he must've dropped on the floor; the orange juice was sitting out with two glasses next to the bottle. Blake never cleaned up after he was cooking. That was always my job, and I didn't mind since I would rather clean than cook any day. Blake had red peppers, onions, green pepper, and ham cut up into pieces on a plate for the omelets. He was stirring the pancake batter in our mixer. And the bacon was on the stove frying. Blake was in a zone; all he did was kiss me on the forehead and went back to turning the bacon, pouring the eggs into the pan and at the same time pouring the batter into the other pan behind the eggs. I picked up all of the garbage and wiped off the counter tops. Blake had his headphones on blasting some song by Drake. I needed to tell Blake that we had to go over to my grandparent's in an hour, but I didn't know how to say it. Blake and my grandmother didn't really see eye to eye. My grandmother just didn't like him. She said he always gave off a weird vibe to her, so even when we had gotten married, she didn't come. She said she didn't want to be in his presence. He knew she didn't like him, so he always stayed away from her. He never liked coming over to hang out with Jean in high school because of her. Then when we started dating he hated picking me up for dates. Also, he didn't like calling the house phone for me; my grandmother made sure he knew that she didn't care for him. So telling him to come with me was always hard, and I knew she didn't know that he was even going to be there today because she would have said no. It was all my grandfather's idea.

I tapped Blake on the shoulder, praying that he would agree to go to my grandparent's house with me. I didn't want to go alone, and I didn't really want to drive. Blake turned around with a big smile on his face. He took his headphones off, turned back around, took the bacon out of the pan, and laid it on the plate with the paper towels on it.

"Blake my grandfather wants you to come with me in an hour to talk about the funeral arrangements. Are you going to come?"

"Janelle you know your grandmother hates me. I really don't want to be there especially now that she's grieving."

24

"Baby come on my grandfather wants the both of us there, and I already told him you would come."

"I don't know why you would tell him that, I do not want to deal with your grandmother today.''

"Well do it for me, baby."

"Janelle no, I am not going."

"Please baby, I need you to come; I need your support."

"My support for what? To pay for everything, you know where my money and credit cards are."

"Are you for real Blake?"

"Yes Janelle, I don't want to be bothered?"

"Not even for Jean, Blake, you won't go for Jean."

"Janelle no. Stop asking me."

It was a week later, and it felt so strange going to my grandmother's house and not seeing Jean. I tried to keep my cool at times, but it was so hard because my grandma always had this look on her face. It always brought me to tears. For about an hour, I sat

with her crying, laughing, and just remembering all of the memories

we had with Jean. I swear it felt like some weights were actually

lifted off of my shoulders. Blake and I didn't really talk about Jeans

death; we kind of strayed away from the conversation. Whenever

Blake did see me crying, he just got a new box a tissue for me. He

would empty the garbage in the bedroom, constantly brought me

food, and made sure I was eating. There were some days when he

stayed home and lay in the bed with me, but then some days he

didn't come home until late and ordered me take out. When he did

come in, he came into the bedroom and would kiss me on the

forehead and then go straight into his office. Those were the days

when I really missed Jean. I hated being home alone knowing my

brother's killer was still walking around free. This person could have

been plotting to kill my grandparents or me, and the police were

probably not even worrying about Jean's case. Thinking about being

murdered or someone breaking in when Blake wasn't home, scared

the hell out of me. I never slept until Blake got home. If he was getting off of work late, I would make sure all of the windows and

doors were locked, and I made sure to keep all of the lights on in the

house because the last few nights I had been terrified of the dark. I

didn't want anyone breaking in, and I wasn't able to see them. I

needed to know who had killed my brother; I needed to know that he

was doing life in prison. I needed my brother's death to get justice. I

wanted them to work a lot harder. Jean at least deserved that.

I was just arriving home from my grandmother's house when

I tried to turn the lock on my door, but at the same time, someone

was turning to come out. I didn't know who that would be since

Blake was at work. I jumped back and started spraying the shadow

in front of me with pepper spray. He started screaming and fell to the

floor. When I looked down, I saw that it was Blake.

"Oh my God, Blake. What are you doing home so early?

You scared the shit out of me."

"Well since it's our anniversary, I thought I would surprise you."

"Aww babe, but I thought you were going to do something tonight?"

"I am, but I thought we would just keep each other company for the rest of the day since I knew how stressed out you have been."

As Blake was trying to get up, my phone started to ring.

"Hello?"

"Yes, is this Janelle Johnson?"

"Yes, this is she."

"Okay, this is Officer Ross. I called you yesterday."

"Oh yes, how are you?"

"Fine, but I have some news."

"Aren't you supposed to be coming over soon?"

"Yes, I was but something came up, and I figured you might want to hear this information," said Officer Ross.

"Oh, what is it?"

I was walking into the house when I heard Blake in the kitchen banging something on the stove. I peeked in and noticed that he was cooking something. I smiled, turned around, and walked into the living room to sit down. Officer Ross was rambling on about some laws, how we could beat the system, and how we could put this situation in the grave if we find out who killed my brother.

"Yes, so Mrs. Johnson someone came up to the police station and told us that the person drove away in a black or blue BMW. The license plate starts with the letter L, but that's all they caught. Since we don't have the rest, we can't really find out who's car that is or anything else. But as soon as we find out more information we will give you a call," Officer Ross said.

"Okay thank you, Officer Ross. That's great news, but I have one question."

"Yes, what is it?"

"If we do find out who it was and I decided not to press charges or anything, will the guy still go to jail even if I ask for them to let him free?"

"That I highly doubt, but we never know. The judge might have a good heart like you, Mrs. Johnson."

"Okay thank you Officer Ross, but can I call you right back?"

"Yes, that would be fine Mrs. Johnson."

I hung up and didn't even say goodbye or thank you. I walked into the kitchen to see what my husband was doing, and he was still in the kitchen cooking something. As I stood in the doorway, he looked up and smiled.

"Janelle you know I love you. And nothing that happens can change that. No matter what I will forever have your back. I remember our wedding day like it was yesterday; I can't believe that it was five years ago. I can't believe it lasted this long since we had so many issues before. But that's the past, and I hope you have forgiven me for it and will continue to love me each and every day."

"Yes, babe I do love you, and yes we have been through so much, but that only continues to keep us stronger. I know we will be together for a very long time and will make our children happy."

"Children?"

"Yes, babe I am pregnant. I was waiting for the right time to tell you, and I thought today would be the perfect time."

Blake ran up to me and put his hands on my belly and started kissing me. I knew Blake loved me and would never hurt me, but for him to kill my brother has got to be a crazy idea. Without a doubt, I knew it was Blake, but for me to even say something now would be crazy.

Chapter 3

Waking up the next morning had to be the worst of them all because I was still wondering when it was going to be my time to be murdered by my husband. Every night, I would go to bed praying to God that I wouldn't be next. I prayed that once I had my baby, Blake didn't feel that's when he should take my life or even the life of our child. I didn't know if I should've believed that it was him or someone else. As I struggle to get out of bed, I noticed that Blake wasn't home, and he didn't even let me know that he had left. I wondered what he was doing up so early on a Saturday when we both were off. Well, since he wasn't home I thought I could go get my hair done and then go food shopping. An hour later, I was out of the shower getting ready to get dressed when Blake was lying on the bed talking on the phone with someone. As I walked past him, I noticed that he had on a blue suit and was really into that phone call. Since I didn't want to disrupt him, I put on my favorite blue jeans, a graphic tee, and my black blazer with my black combat boots. I tied my curly wet hair in a bun and walked out the door. As I got into Blake's BMW, I saw him at the door waving me down to come back inside the house. My heart started beating fast. I thought I could see it coming out of my shirt.

"What's up babe?" I asked.

"Nothing, where you going?"

"To the grocery store, then to get my hair done. Why, do you want to come?"

"Nah, you know I hate sitting in that hair salon waiting for you. But when you go out, can you pick up some heavy duty garbage bags for the garage, a new rake, and a shovel."

" Yeah babe, but don't we already have a new shovel in the garage?"

"We did, but I don't know what happened to it. It was there a month ago. Someone must've stole it."

33

"Damn, something's always getting stolen from our yard. I think it's time we move out anyway so we can get the baby's room done before I go into labor."

"Babe, now you're rushing your pregnancy. I am not ready for the baby to be here yet," said Blake.

"Okay babe, I'll be back later on. I love you." I replied.

"I love you too baby." As Blake leaned in to kiss me, I wanted to back up, but I didn't want to make anything awkward.

As I was driving to the grocery store, the detective from my brother's case called me letting me know some good information.

"Hey Janelle, I have some news for you," said the detective.

"Yeah, what is it?" I asked curiously.

"We initially thought that it was a man who killed your brother. We just found out that it was a female because when we ran more tests, we came across a scratch on his head. This scratch was made by an acrylic nail."

"So you're telling me that this person was a female? I asked confused.

"Yes, I don't know how that is possible. But whoever this girl was, he must've done her dirty, and she wanted her revenge."

Right away, I thought about his ex-girlfriend, Brandi. This girl was in love with my brother and after they broke up she would always do crazy things to his car or to him.

"Okay, thank you Officer Ross. I'll talk to you later."

"Okay, bye Janelle."

I hung up. Since I wasn't in the mood to go and get my hair done anymore, I went to see if I could find Brandi anywhere in our old neighborhood. Once I got to Peach Street, I saw her standing on the side of the road waiting for the bus with her kids. I pulled over, and the next thing I knew, she was in the car with me heading to the diner on Second Avenue. Brandi was acting really strange. She talking but seemed very nervous.

"I am so sorry about Jean girl; Jean was such a good man. I remember when we were dating. He was so good to me.

"So Brandi, were you around the night my brother was shot? I never got a chance to talk to you the night of the wake." Brandi continued to act as if she was keeping something from me.

"Brandi, are you listening?

"Yes, I actually was," she announced in a low tone. I turned to look at her briefly. Then I turned my eyes back to the road.

She continued, "I was walking home from work when I saw this female walking up behind your brother with a gun in her hand, and as I screamed out to your brother, it was too late. She had shot him, and I took off running because I didn't want her to come and find me."

Brandi began to sob. As I sat listening to her, I started crying as well. I could no longer see the road, hear her kids yelling, or notice that I had hit a tree. I just sat there crying. My chest was hurting, my head was pounding, and my face was drenched with tears. I just wanted to be wrapped up in Blake's arms right then. All I could hear was Brandi screaming, "Janelle." I was trying so hard to stop crying, but I couldn't. I felt my chest getting tight, and I started to lose my breath. I was gasping for air when I realized that my asthma pump was in the truck, and I was in Blake's car.

"I was just in a car accident, and my friend is having an asthma attack. She doesn't have her pump with her. Please hurry up and get here." Brandi screamed into the phone.

"Ma'am I need you to calm down. Where exactly are you?" the operator asked.

"I'm off of Jericho Turnpike by the TD Bank; please come fast. I don't think she's going to make it," said Brandi frightened.

I woke up in the hospital with wires in my nose, IV's in the arm and hand, and I had on a neck brace. I looked up and saw Blake pacing the floor, biting his nails. I hadn't seen Blake so emotional since his mom had passed a few months before. He looked like he just put on anything when he found out what had happened. He had on a long sleeve shirt with his cargo shorts, his work socks, and his house slippers. All I could do was laugh and even that hurt. He turned around, and his face lit up quickly. He had the biggest smile on his face, and when I smiled, he came up to me and kissed me. I swear that felt so good. I really needed to be loved for just one second, and his lips were all that I needed.

"Babe, how are you feeling? I was so worried about you. I didn't think you were going to make it when Brandi called me and told me what had happened."

"Wait, baby how are Brandi's children?" I tried getting up, but as soon as I lifted my head, I was dizzy.

"Oh yeah they're fine, the little one just broke her leg. Other than that, she's fine. Brandi was up here, but you were asleep, and she said she would come back once you were awake."

"Oh my God, babe I feel so bad. If only I was watching where I was going, I would have seen that tree."

"Baby, don't go blaming yourself; you were emotional. Don't go stressing yourself out about something as small as that. Be grateful all of you guys are alive, especially since you didn't have your pump. You really could be dead right now," said Blake.

After being in the hospital for about four hours, I couldn't help but feel bad about what I did to Brandi and her children. I wasn't supposed to leave my room because Blake didn't want me to get up. He wanted me to rest, but I had done enough resting. I needed to go and check up on Brandi and her children. I needed to know for sure that they were okay. I needed to make sure she wasn't trying to sue me. Blake was laying in the bed next to me. He still had on the same clothes that I had seen him in earlier. He was snoring loud, and I could see that he had turned his phone on vibrate because his phone kept blinking like he had messages. I know it could only be work since that was the only thing he used his phone for.

Sometimes that bothered me. I hated when we would be at dinner for

our anniversary or even just during date night, and he would pick up

his phone at the table and would talk the whole time we were there.

There was even a time when he got up from the table and left his

wallet so I could pay for dinner. That day was one of the worst

birthdays with him ever. After that, I vowed that we would never go

out to eat on my birthday. And ever since then, we stay at home, and

he cooks me dinner, so whenever his phone rings he can answer it

and finish cooking at the same time, and it wouldn't be rude to the

other people in restaurants.

The nurses at the nurse's station were sitting around talking.

They weren't paying me any attention. I hated coming to this

hospital because the nurses were ghetto, rude and didn't do their job.

They expected to get paid to do absolutely nothing. By the time I got

over to the nurse's station rolling my IV and trying to cover my

underwear, I saw Brandi down the hall walking with a pitcher of ice.

She looked like she was fine. She didn't have on a hospital gown, so

she seemed to be okay, but who was Brandi getting ice for when her daughter was in the pediatrics wing. I slowly walked on the cold

hospital floor in my thick yellow socks with the rubber on the

bottom so I wouldn't fall. I noticed that it was extremely quiet, no

one was screaming for a nurse, I didn't hear anyone coughing, or

moaning. It seemed like everyone had died, and I was the only sick

one here. It was strange because most hospitals were busy with

patients; it wasn't that late. It was only eight-thirty. I know most of

the people's visitors had left, but even the patients were quiet.

I thought Brandi would be on another floor since it was her

daughter who was admitted and she was fine walking around getting

pitchers of ice. When I reached the room that I saw Brandi walk

into, I could hear someone else's voice in the background. I wasn't

sure if she was on the phone or if there was someone else there. It

wasn't her daughter's voice. What I heard was a man's voice. I felt

like I had heard that voice before, but I couldn't tell. I walked into

the room, and Brandi was sitting by the window drinking a cup of

water. Her daughter was sleeping. She was covered in about three

hospital blankets, and her leg was propped up on two pillows. When

I walked in, Brandi didn't notice me at first, she kept on looking out of the window. I didn't see anyone else in the room, so she must've been on the phone or something. I walked over to the bed where her daughter was sleeping; she had the remote in her hand, and her hair was brushed back into a bun. When I looked over, I saw Brandi staring at me smiling. She didn't say a word until I was about to say something and she stopped me.

"I know what you're going to say and there's no need for it. Anyway, Javaeah has always wanted to break her leg, and you did that for her. You should have heard her in here earlier. She was so excited. Crazy right? But I don't blame you, Janelle. I am so sorry; I should have told you sooner. I hope you can forgive me?"

"No Brandi, I am sorry, I put your whole family in danger. Please forgive me." Brandi stood up and walked over to where I was sitting. She touched my shoulder. I looked back down at her daughter, and she was snoring.

"I know you can't wait to have your own someday."

"Yes, I can't wait. Blake and I want to have a baby, but we are just going to let it happen. Planning a baby makes things a lot more difficult."

"Yes it does girl, I remember when Michael and I were trying. We tried for a year, and we couldn't get pregnant until this one night we both were at my friend's wedding and were crazy drunk. We got home that night and had sex, forgetting that we were planning, and a month later, I had found out I was pregnant. It was the happiest time of my life. We both were very excited. It's such a good feeling."

"I bet it was. But I should go Brandi; I'll let you get some rest."

I didn't think it was necessary to tell her that I was already pregnant because I didn't want her in my business anyway.

Chapter 4

After we had left the hospital, we dropped off Brandi and her daughter. It was a little chilly outside. Blake and I listened to a bunch of old R&B music the rest of the ride home from Brandi's. I didn't want to speak on anything that was going on. I didn't know if I should tell Blake about what the detective had told me, which caused me to get us here in the first place. I didn't know who else to tell because if I was to tell my grandparents that would probably destroy them, and I didn't want them to suffer anymore. We continued home in peace and quiet.

Months had passed since leaving the hospital, the baby was kicking for the first time; it was weird to feel the kick. I was now six months going on seven, and he was just now kicking me. There would be times when he moved around, but this time it was different. He was forcefully moving. He was kicking me for most of

44

the ride. I was going to wait to tell Blake about it and let him feel

him later if he was to kick me again, but who knew if this would

stop by the time we got home. I put my hand on my stomach and he

kicked me harder, I could see and feel his foot through my shirt. He

must've been stretching. Blake and I were headed home from one of

my doctor's appointments.

"Blake oh my God, feel this, hurry up. Give me your hand."

"Baby, what are you talking about? I'm driving. Do I need to

go back to the doctor?"

"No, give me your hand."

Blake moved his right hand off of the steering wheel, and I

put his hand where the baby was kicking. Blake could feel his foot

pushing on my stomach. Blake's hand covered most of my belly so

when the baby did move around, he felt it from the top to right

below my belly button. Blake's hand never moved off of my

stomach; he just kept it there while we were still on our way back

home.

"Nelly I can't believe that he's moving so much. This is the first time I've ever felt him moving."

"I know, me too, the doctor did say that nothing was wrong and we would feel him when he did decide to move. I am just glad that he did finally move."

"Yeah, me too because I thought something was wrong with him."

Before I knew it, we were pulling into the driveway; the sun was going down. I was starving, I was hoping Blake would cook something for dinner. He probably would if I asked him, but I knew he was tired from working and being at the doctor with me. Blake jumped out of the car and ran over to help me out of the car. He was grabbing my arm and helping me get out as if I couldn't walk. I knew he only wanted to protect me, but I needed him not to worry so much. I was fine. When we got into the house, Blake helped me get up the steps to the bedroom; he led me to the bed and helped me take off my boots. My feet were swollen, and it felt good to finally take off my shoes. I got off of the bed and went into the bathroom to brush my teeth when I heard Blake on the phone in his office. He was talking to someone on speaker. I could faintly hear a guy's voice, but I couldn't make out what he was talking about. The guy on the phone was talking about some kind of pills that he had given Blake and was asking if the pill had started working. I didn't hear Blake answer him and that's when I decided to go and see who Blake was talking too. I slowly walked to the back of the house toward Blake's office when he said everything was working fine, and he would visit him soon. This time around Blake was taking down some numbers, which wasn't a phone number because he repeated sixteen numbers and three letters. I didn't know what the hell that stood for, but I knew it wasn't something that involved me. I got closer to the door and poked my head in; Blake looked up and smiled. He whispered, "What's up?" I asked him if he wanted me to order out. He shook his head, yes. I then exited the room.

This was very strange of Blake. Now that I had suspected that Blake had murdered my brother, I was more worried about who he was talking to and everything he did that supposedly involved work. I knew he was acquainted with a lot of people, and I knew a lot of people from his old neighborhood always needed him for help, but I didn't know what else he did when he was in his office or even when he was out for business. I wanted to ask him about where he was the night of my brother's death and why he was up late that night eating in the dining room. Blake usually never eats down there unless we have family over or when he plans to cook new dishes. We normally eat in the bedroom or on the sofa in the living room. So that was the first thing that was different, and now him and the strange phone calls with people. I wanted to believe that Blake was not the one and that the person who told the police about the BMW was wrong. I was hoping they had really seen a black Nissan Altima instead. I wanted the detective to call me and tell me that the information they had was not correct, and they were taking the case a lot more serious after finding out that the information was wrong. I was trying to figure out how they found traces of acrylic nails in his skin. How and why would Blake get his nails done or better yet who would he be blaming this murder on? Who did he want to go to jail for his actions? I just didn't know, and I couldn't even believe that Blake was capable of anything like that. And why would he kill my brother when they were practically brothers back in the day? When we all were in high school, Jean and Blake were so close they would tell everyone who asked that they were half-brothers, so I don't think that he would kill him after their dispute.

Laying on the sofa waiting for the delivery guy to come, I was flicking through the TV channels when Blake came down the steps. He had changed into a pair of basketball shorts and was carrying a notebook. It looked like Blake's work planner. He walked straight into the kitchen. I could hear him in the cabinets looking for a glass, and he was washing it out. Blake had this thing where he had to always rewash a clean cup each time he went to use it. Blake did this every time he wanted to use a cup in the house.

"Janelle baby, do you want something to drink?"

"Yes, can I get a glass of cranberry juice?"

"Okay babe, what did you order?"

49

"Pizza, I was craving buffalo wings and pepperoni."

"Babe we just had pizza two nights ago."

"I know, but I was craving wings."

"I could have just made you some wings."

"So what did you want? Chinese?"

"No babe, I want whatever you want."

"Really, shut up, what did you want?"

"I'll order it now?"

"I'll eat the pizza and wings you ordered."

"Who said I ordered wings for you. I said I was craving wings."

Blake came walking into the living room holding two glasses of cranberry juice. He sat down next to me on the sofa and grabbed the remote off of the table. He was switching through the TV channels and finally stopped when he came to a movie that looked interesting. It had just started, which was good because we hated watching movies after they had already begun. I didn't know what this movie was about, but it seemed good. Blake didn't really speak much, he just watched the movie, sometimes he would make comments about how dumb the characters were, but we didn't really talk at all. The whole time I couldn't keep myself awake, I was trying, but I was freezing and exhausted. The movie was extremely boring, but Blake was enjoying it. I didn't get any of the jokes they made, nor did I think it was good overall. So I got up from the sofa and took our empty glasses and plates to the kitchen. When I got back into the living room, Blake had turned the TV off and was no longer on the sofa. I didn't even hear him. I walked upstairs to the bedroom and Blake was already in the bed reading a book. He lay on top of the blankets in his shorts. I took off my clothes and changed into my silk nightgown and climbed in the bed next to him. He didn't go to bed right away; we kissed and said our good nights.

Chapter 5

I woke up to sharp pains; they must've been contractions. I laid there for a few minutes waiting for the next one to happen. It was ten minutes before I felt the next contraction. This time it had gotten slightly worse than before. I turned on my back and began to rub my belly. I wasn't sure if I was having labor contractions or Braxton Hick's. It was four in the morning, and usually Blake would be getting ready for work because he drives to Pennsylvania on Thursdays meetings with some other law firm company. They were going to be moving part of the business there, and there was a chance we would've had to move, but Blake was fighting it because of my brother's death and us having a baby. But I knew that Blake really wanted to move. He loved to travel for work, and I didn't want to move to Alabama and leave my grandparents. I know he hated me for that decision. At the time, it was the right thing to do. I was still going to college. I had five more classes to take, and then I

52

was supposed to intern in one of the hospitals in New York City. That was the plan, and I didn't want to move while completing my education. I ended up finishing school and becoming a doctor. I did, however, only finish my education and didn't start working right away. Right before my brother died, I quit my job. I was looking for a job close to home, but my dream was to open my own urgent care facility for the inner city communities that had Medicare and Medicaid insurance or didn't have any at all. I wanted to help minorities and to give them the medical treatment they needed and deserved. But I didn't get a chance to do any of that.

Ten more minutes had gone by, and another contraction hit me. I had never felt pain like this in my life. I wasn't due for another three months. I was worried because it was too early to have this baby.

"Blake wake up. Wake up."

"What?''

"I think I am going into labor; I'm having contractions."

"Are you serious, Janelle?"

"Baby I am sure."

"It's probably just gas; you did eat all ten buffalo wings."

"Baby I am serious. I am having contractions every ten minutes. I think we should go to the emergency room."

Blake got up from the bed, threw on a pair of sweats, and grabbed my packed bag out of the closet. I tried to get up, but I was in so much pain. By the time I made it to the stairs, my water had broke, and Blake was running around downstairs trying to find the car keys. I could hear him cursing, breathing hard, and sighing. I turned around, grabbed my keys out of my purse in the bedroom, and made my way down the steps. I didn't see Blake in the house so he must've been outside. Blake had all of the lights on, and the pillows on the sofa were on the floor. He was really panicking, and it wasn't good because he had to drive us to the hospital. I knew Blake would panic when I went into labor because it's our first child. I also knew if I were to go in labor early like now, it would cause him to lose his mind. I wasn't anywhere near my due date. That was scary because I didn't want anything to be wrong with my child. Premature birth is terrifying. You never know what's going to happen.

When I walked outside, I gave Blake the keys to my truck, and we made our way to the hospital. The whole time I was thinking about Jean and his death. I missed my brother every single day and even more at that moment because he wasn't there to see my son. He was either in Heaven or Hell. The thought of my brother screaming from Hell frightened me. I didn't want to even imagine it. I closed my eyes and tried to breathe through the pains of the contractions. They were coming a lot closer now, and I could no longer bare the pain. They were worse than earlier. It felt like we were driving forever. Blake was speeding on the highway like the rest of the cars on their way to work. It was still dark out, but there were a lot of cars on the road. We were heading to the hospital where my doctor worked since he had been monitoring me this whole time. It didn't feel right going anywhere else, and since I was going into labor before my actual due date, we should have gone to the hospital closer to the house. But we wanted my regular doctor to deliver the baby. We were prepared to take the trip then, but at the moment I was regretting everything. It felt like he was already making his way out and we still had two more exits. The hospital was three more miles once we reach the exit. The longer it took to get there, my contractions were getting worse and worse by the minute. I knew the baby was coming.

We finally reached the hospital, and my doctor was waiting in the emergency room with a wheelchair. He was shocked that I was coming in this early. He had warned me that I might go into early labor, so he always made sure the baby was healthy and ready to come. I wasn't sure what was going to happen once I got into a room, but I knew I was ready for it. Blake was calling my grandparents, his sister, and my cousin, Autumn, to let them know the baby might be coming sooner than planned. He was in a panic. For the first twenty minutes, they waited for my contractions to get closer and then once it was time, I was in position to deliver. By that point, I was terrified. I was about to be a mother, about to see my baby boy. I was going to have to see him suffer if he had any problems. Blake was standing next to me holding my hand when the doctor came into the room. He was about to check on me when his phone rang. He let go of my hand and answered it. He walked into the hallway, and when he came back, he had a huge smile on his face. I couldn't believe that he had taken a work call when I was about to give birth to his son. I wanted to slap the shit out of him, but then I realized I shouldn't be angry and that I should just focus on giving birth. My doctor interrupted me and told me that I was going to need a C-section due to the baby's position. I really didn't want to have a major cut like that. I wanted to push him out naturally.

They wheeled me into a different room, and there were a ton of other nurses inside. They hooked me up to some wires, and the only thing I remember was my lower body going numb. I faintly recall seeing the baby, but after that everything went black. I woke up in my room, and my grandmother was there sitting next to Blake and my grandfather. It was such a happy sight, seeing them all in the same room together. They were bonding; my grandmother was smiling and laughing with Blake, which she never does. I thought this day would never come, but it did. I didn't want to interrupt them, so I closed my eyes and tried to get some rest. My body was in so much pain. I felt a little uneasy. Something was different with my body. My head was hurting, and I felt like things were different. I could hear them in the background talking and enjoying each other, but I couldn't concentrate on them. My mind was somewhere else. I drifted off to sleep dreaming about my brother's death.

At first, I was standing in front of my house watching Jean walk inside, I was staring at him talking to Blake at the door. They were both laughing and then I had come outside carrying a baby girl. The next couple of minutes we were in the dining room eating dinner and Blake had left to put the baby in her crib upstairs. Jean and I were talking about killing someone. Jean kept on telling me to kill someone and how that was the right thing to do. He was telling me to use certain weapons and how and when to do it. We never talked about who, but we both knew deep down inside. Jean was looking around to make sure that Blake wasn't coming down yet. He then passed me a piece of black paper from his pocket and told me not to lose it. The paper had all of the items I needed to buy. The person's name and address was on it and who I was supposed to call once I had finished the task. Blake had come back down carrying a notebook. He opened the book and laid it out on the table; there was a map inside. The paper was covered in something red, which appeared to be blood. We all had looked at each other not saying a word. I then took the book out of Blake's hands and went through the rest of it. Blake had the bloody map in his hands, and Jean was laughing. He was laughing so hard that tears were forming from his eyes. The pages in the book were empty except for the last page which read: KILL ME NOW, OR I WILL GET YOU FIRST. I didn't know what that meant, but we all looked at each other confused and ended up putting the stuff away and continuing dinner. I was about to get up and walk to the kitchen for another cup of wine when I woke up from the dream and Blake was standing over me.

He was holding me down on the bed; I could see my grandmother in one corner holding Junior in her hands. My grandfather was holding down my legs. Blake was screaming, asking for a nurse to come in the room. I felt my body getting hot; I was sweating, trying to fight them off of me. I was biting and scratching at Blake's face. Blake had a few scratches on his face, and my grandfather was praying. While he was holding my feet, I could hear my grandmother in the background screaming Jesus. She was yelling Jesus so loud I thought I had seen the light. The next thing I knew a few doctors and nurses came in and restrained my arms and legs. I was pinned down while they took each leg and arm and tied them to the hospital bed. Once they had me tied down, one of the nurses took Junior out of the room. My grandmother was pacing back and forth, and Blake was rubbing my left hand. He was sitting on the bed confused; he didn't move at all.

"I will kill you, Blake. You are not the guy you say you are."

"Janelle, what are you talking about?"

"You know what I am talking about. Don't play stupid."

"Janelle, why do you want to kill me?"

"Because you hurt me, you are evil."

"Janelle baby."

"Don't call me baby, you devil. You try to fool everyone by making them believe you're such a hero, but boy you are not fooling anyone but yourself."

"Please Janelle."

Blake looked over at my grandparents and got up and left the room. I continued to talk about Blakes evil intentions, and each time a new doctor had come in to check on me. For a long time, Blake and my grandparents were walking in and out of the room, and then it stopped. They all had left except for Blake. After returning to the room, he remained next to me the whole time. He never got up from the bed again. While Blake and a few doctors were talking, one of the nurses came in and injected me with something that burned. My entire arm was on fire. I was screaming at the top of my lungs, but no one seemed to hear me. They didn't turn around nor did the nurse ask if I was okay.

"Blake?"

He turned around and looked at me; the doctor took out his notepad and pen. He was waiting for me to speak to write it all down.

"Blake, why am I tied to the bed, what the hell is going on?"

"Janelle?"

"Blake, what is going on?"

"Are you okay? You don't remember what happened?" Blake and the doctor both stepped closer to me.

"All I remember is going into labor. Did we lose him? Oh my god Blake, please don't tell me."

"Babe, no he is safe, he's healthy. But do you remember anything else?"

"No, what happened."

Everything went black; then I woke up to them wheeling me out of the room. Blake had all of our belongings. I didn't know where I was going until I heard someone say they were taking me to a mental institution. I heard them say, "They don't handle my kind of problem here."

Chapter 6

Waking up in a mental institution has got to be the worse feeling ever, but it was a little better than sitting in jail. I still didn't understand why they were here running all of these tests and giving me medications I'd never heard of. They watched me like a hawk. I was placed in a white room with one tiny window that had bars on both the inside and the outside. I wasn't allowed to get any fresh air nor listen to the rain when it poured. It had been about 39 days since the day I went into labor and accused Blake of being a horrible man. My mind was kind of fuzzy from that night; I only remember being wheeled out of the hospital into a van while they put a restraint jacket on me. I honestly am afraid of the thought of what would have happened if I would have hurt him. The idea of that made me nauseous, and I had to keep my focus on the black dot on the ceiling that looked more like a rain cloud each day. I'd spent the last 39 days eating foods that were bland and boring. No matter how much I refused to eat, they force fed me. I felt like I was being forced

against my will to be or do something that was me, but when I really

thought it, I didn't really know myself because I was sitting in there.

I couldn't understand a word the doctors were saying. I hated how

they wouldn't tell me anything. All I wanted to know was if I could

see my family or at least talk to the love of my life. I wondered if

Blake has even tried to call me or if he even cared. I wanted to

know how he felt about the whole thing. I wondered if he was

having a hard time taking care of the baby or if he hired someone to

take care of him while he worked. I don't know how all of this could

have happened in a matter of a month. I couldn't believe that was

going to be my life. I was curious about how I would act, feel, or

even live after returning home. I wanted it all to be over with so that

I could just live my life with my family. What if I didn't leave until

junior was 13 or something? I didn't want him to know me as his

crazy mother and be afraid of me or even hate me. As I sat there and

began to cry, I noticed that someone was looking into my room and

was writing things down. I couldn't help but wonder what they were writing down. Had this other person come out at night and I didn't even notice? Was this individual my alter ego? Was she planning her next attempt to ruin my life? I needed to get some answers, and I didn't know how I was going to get them. I needed to find a way to communicate with her or at least on how to get inside my own mind.

Waking up to another horrible breakfast and another three pills that I could hardly swallow was the way I started every morning. They would wake me up at 8:00 a.m. and let me sit and watch the news for an hour or take a shower without any assistance, but that didn't happen too often. I usually wrote letters to Blake every day and kept them in my nightstand until they allowed me to communicate with people who weren't like me. Wow, that sounds awkward. *People like me.* Yeah, never thought I'd be saying those words. Sitting on the pale flower sofa brought back memories of my childhood. My grandmother used to have one, but she always kept her living room furniture in plastic. It was horrible plastic that we would get stuck to on hot summer days, or we slid off of when we wore something silky. I remember the days when my grandfather would come home from his doctor's appointments. He would always be so tired after dialysis, but he always made time to play with Jean and I. He made up this game called *"Hot Lava."* The whole object of the game was to not slip off of the sofa, but we had to wear our grandmother's silk pajamas. The funny thing is that he always won. He never once slipped off of the couch.

"Janelle, we need you in the evaluation room; it's time to run a few tests."

I got up and walked over to the back of the building noticing how this guy was sitting in the corner yelling at himself; he was having a full argument. I started to wonder if that was how I acted at times. Had I ever talked to myself? Had anyone noticed my strange behavior? As I stood and watched, this man continue to ramble on about how he wanted to eat chicken and how the other one wanted steak, I remembered a time when I was dating this guy back in high school, and we had gotten into an argument about prom or something. He said that I was acting funny. I didn't understand what he meant, but he called me bipolar. I still didn't understand or even notice what he was talking about until that moment, and I still was not so sure.

"JANELLE, PLEASE COME TO THE EVALUATION ROOM!" I heard a lady calling me on the loud speaker. As I walked a lot faster to the room, I started to get nervous and didn't know what to expect since that was my first time having to talk to someone.

"Hello Janelle, come in. Take a seat and relax." As I sat down on the couch, the psychiatrist was wearing a black and white pinstriped pencil skirt with an off-white collared shirt. She had on old penny loafers that looked like she got them 12 years ago and didn't want to buy new ones because those were comfortable. She wore her glasses on the tip of her nose so I could notice her light green eyes and that one lazy eye. I tried my best not to stare at her too hard, but she was so distracting.

"How are you doing? I'm assuming you are doing well. You are one of the quiet ones here". "Yeah, I'm fine, just taking it day by day. I still don't know why I am here exactly. I was actually wondering if you could tell me what happened the night I was admitted here."

"Well Janelle, that night you said you wanted to kill your husband." I looked at her waiting for more, but she was staring at me waiting for me to react or something.

"Okay but what else happened? Was anyone hurt? Did I cause a scene? Did you guys notice a change since then? I really would like to have some answers."

"Janelle sweetie, I don't know most of the answers to the questions you are asking, but I do know when you came in here you were perfectly fine. We are really trying to understand what caused you to act out."

I lay back on the dark brown leather sofa and thought about my family. The doctor came in a few minutes later and told me he was going to run a few tests. The doctor was this tall white guy with blonde hair, he had a deep tanned complexion, and he was dressed in jeans and a t-shirt. He was actually very handsome. He had this unique "swagger" about himself that made me feel nervous. "Hey Janelle, how are you today?"

"I'm fine, but what exactly are we doing today?"

"We will be performing an electroencephalogram on you, and then we will send you back to your room."

"So, you will have the results tomorrow?"

"Yes we will, and that will determine how your brain works or if something is wrong."

"Okay Doctor?"

"Oh, I'm sorry Doctor Landry.''

As Doctor Landry began to hook me up to the machine, I felt myself drifting off to sleep thinking about being with my family. A few minutes later, I awoke and looked up at him. I felt really strange. It felt as if I had dreamed that I was talking to someone, but I was someone else. It seemed as if I was far away. Dr. Landry was looking at me with great concern. Then he started to explain my conversation with him during that time. He reported that I was acting very strange and our conversation was not a normal one. He looked very uncomfortable as he repeated our conversation to me.

"When you came in for more testing, you fell asleep. When you awoke, you started speaking, but it wasn't really you. Let me start from the beginning. You begin speaking."

"Doctor Landry? It's me, Sasha." He explained that he then looked around to see if there was someone at the door. Then he looked down at me.

"Sasha?" He stated.

"Yes it's me, the girl you all have been waiting for."

"No you are not Sasha, you are Janelle." He responded confused.

"Who is Janelle? I don't know her. She's gone.''

"Okay, Sasha. What can I help you with today?"

"I need a favor."

71

He then said that I tried to get up, but he forced me to lie back down so that I wouldn't mess up the wires.

Doctor Landry removed the wires, He explained that he turned off the machine after that and took a seat in front of me. I continued to say that I was Sasha. He then stated,

"So, Sasha what kind of favor do you need?"

"I need someone to talk to; I was waiting for you to talk to me because I don't feel comfortable talking to the psychiatrist here." Doctor Landry explained that he picked up the notebook on the table next to him and began writing down our conversation.

"How was your childhood Janelle? … I mean Sasha." He said.

"My childhood .."

He said that looked up at the ceiling and began to cry before I continued.

"My childhood was good; you know like every other kid's childhood. The regular beatings, parents arguing, Daddy hitting Mommy, and yeah I can't forget about my uncle touching me. "And how do you feel now about the way you lived your childhood?"

He continued.

"Doctor Landry, how was your childhood?"

"It was good Sasha. I lived with my mom and dad, I have two brothers, and we were a middle-class family. So Sasha how did you feel about your parents?

"I loved my parents; they gave me and my brother the world."

Dr. Landry explained that I got quiet at that point and began to rub my hands together. I looked at him with tears in my eyes before I continued. I knew this was going to be a long night because I saw the hurt that she felt.

"Doctor Landry you have to promise me that you will not and when I say not I mean not tell anyone this. Do you promise?"

"I promise Sasha."

Dr. Landry said I then immediately came out of what seemed like a trance and stared up at him.

"Okay doctor Landry but I killed my …. My brother."

Chapter 7

I was waiting in my room when one of the nurses came in and told me that my husband was in the waiting room. I was shocked that I threw on a little chapstick since I wasn't allowed to have anything else. I was so excited about being able to see him that I didn't even care how I looked. When I saw him carrying my favorite flowers, he had the biggest smile on his face, and I could see his gums. Walking across the room, I started to cry because I missed him so much and all the love I thought that would vanish came rushing back. My body got hot, and all I wanted to do was make love to him and apologize. It was difficult seeing him without our son, but I had to hold back the tears and face reality. Once I got close enough to him, we hugged, and I felt his heartbeat. It felt good to be able to feel his heart because at least one of us could have a regular heartbeat. I took a step back after we hugged. I looked up at him, and he was staring at me with so much confusion. He then leaned in and kissed me. It was so passionate that I felt my legs get weak, and I had to step back and smile. He was all I had wanted for the past few months and having him there, knowing he still felt the same way about me, made me feel a lot better about my situation. My rock had come, and that's all that mattered.

"Baby I missed you so much. How are you?" said Blake.

"I'm good baby; I missed you so much. I can't believe you're actually here."

"I know babe, but you know I love you and wouldn't leave you alone especially when you need me more than ever before." Those words rolled off of his tongue so well.

"How's Junior doing?"

"He's good Janelle; he's with the babysitter."

I looked out of the window that was behind Blake and thought about how my son was getting to know the babysitter and not his own mother.

"Babe? What are you thinking about?" asked Blake.

"Baby … I'm sorry, I didn't mean to hurt you."

"Janelle stop apologizing, it's not your fault. I love you; I'm here for you. Now tell me how the food here is?" We both started laughing.

"Horrible, I'd rather starve."

"And what good would that be if you die here and not come home to your family."

"Baby … I have something to tell you; I just want you to understand and not judge me. It's not easy to say or easy for me to process right now but I'm just going to say it. I …" Blake stopped me and kissed me. I pushed him away knowing I wanted it. I just felt it wasn't the right time for him to comfort me since I was about to tell him that I was a killer and couldn't stop it even if I had tried. When I found out that I had killed my parents, I didn't know how to feel at all. I started to think that maybe I was also the one who murdered my brother.

"Blake baby please sit down. I really need to tell you the truth," said Janelle.

"Did you find someone else?"

Blake had this smirk on his face that expressed he was joking, but I didn't smile. I just looked at him.

"Blake I am being serious right now. Stop with the jokes for a second."

Blake put his head down.

"Blake I don't know how you're going to take this, but I have to tell you something that might change your mind about me. I love you and you know I would never try to do anything to anyone when I am in the right state of mind."

"Yes I know baby, what's up? What do you have to tell me?" asked Blake.

"I killed my parents."

I looked away so that I didn't have to see Blake's facial expression. For a second it was so quiet, I thought I was actually alone. Blake didn't move, talk, or breathe. He was shocked; he didn't know what to do. We looked at each other both wondering which one of us was going to speak first or if I was going to react in a way he didn't want to see. After about ten minutes of us staring at each other, I got up from the sofa to walk back to my room. Blake jumped up from that spot and called my name. I didn't want to turn around because I didn't want him to see the tears that had gradually begin to form at the surface of my eyes. It was really hard to see him because I was trying not to let any tears hit my cheeks and because of that my eyelashes became soaked and blinded me.

"Janelle. Turn around. I need to see your face," Blake exclaimed.

I turned around using my gray long sleeve shirt to wipe away the tears that fell down my cheeks. Blake walked over to where I was standing, grabbed my arm, pulled me in close and kissed me. That was when I knew the love of my life would support me no matter what.

"Janelle don't you worry about what happened in the past. I know you're hurting because you can't seem to trust yourself or even believe what you have done. I know this is a lot for you, as for myself, but baby keep your head up. I'm not going anywhere, and I will get you all the help you need. I love you, and nothing will change that."

 I hugged him so tight I didn't want to let him go. He was so warm; he seemed to be warmer with every touch, yet I felt so cold.

"I love you, Blake."

"I love you too."

Blake had been gone a few hours, and I was laying in my bed thinking about how I had gotten to that point. I needed answers; I needed to know when this disorder started. Who else had this in my family, would my son develop it? I was so focused on figuring out how I got to this point; I didn't even realize that I had fallen asleep. I

80

woke up to another three pills and a cup of orange juice. For breakfast, they actually gave us something good. I ate pancakes, eggs, corn beef hash, and drank some hot tea. It was delicious. I felt like I was at home. I mean my actual home in bed, wearing my robe and fuzzy socks, wearing my wedding ring and playing with my son. I really needed to get better so that I could go on home and live a somewhat normal life. I was sitting down at the table watching the news when this guy walked up asking to sit down. There were a bunch of other available tables, but he had to ask to sit with me. I didn't want to be rude about it, so I just let him sit there. As I minded my business, I caught him staring at me. It was an awkward stare, like he wanted to say something but didn't know how, making it more uncomfortable than it already was.

"Hi, I'm Janelle. I haven't seen you before, are you new?"

"Hi, I'm Darrel, and yes I was admitted early this morning."

"Well, I see you're not that crazy figuring that you're not locked up in your room and being forced pills. Nice meeting you."

I looked back up at the TV to listen to what the president had to say about going to war with Siberia.

"I may have a multiple personality disorder, but I'm not crazy. A loose screw here and there, but I'm far from crazy. You must be crazy."

"I'm not crazy; I'm just like you."

I looked him in the eyes to read him because he reminded me of someone I knew when I was in high school.

"Why do you think that?" asked Darrel.

"Well for starters we both have multiple personality disorder; we might be on the same level. You seem to not understand exactly why you are here and just want to get out."

"Wrong. You are so wrong sunshine."

I looked out of the window next to me.

"Don't look away, I see you. I can tell you miss your family. You had a real life outside of this place. That was me before the first time I was here."

"You were here before?"

"Yes."

"Why? If you don't mind me asking."

"Nah I don't. When I first found out that I had multiple personality disorder, I wasn't in the right frame of mind. I was locked in my room for 13 months and 4 days. It was the worst year of my life. I thought losing my job was worse until I came here. They treat you good here, but when you don't know you're here or how you got here, you tend to create other things in your head."

"I know what you mean, well I wasn't in my room for that long, but it felt like it."

"So tell me, Janelle, what's your story?" asked Darrel.

"What do you mean?"

"Listen, we all have a story. From how we got here, to why it happened the way it did, and how we ended up in this hospital."

"Oh, that story."

"Yeah, that story."

"Well, I tried to kill my husband the night I ended up here; I don't remember too much of it because the girl, Sasha, took over. She also came out to tell the doctor how I killed my parents when I was a child. And that's all I know."

"Really? Hm."

"What?" I asked.

"Nothing, relax sunshine," said Darrel.

"So what's your story?" I asked Darrel.

"Well, I found out I had this disorder when I was 11 years old. I had an addiction to fire; I lit anything I could get my hands on. I only lit things on fire after school around 7 p.m. when Jake seemed

84

to want to come out. Sometimes I would sneak out of the house and light toads on fire."

"Wait, wait, wait, so you're telling me you lit things on fire up until now?"

"Yes, it's weird I know."

"Yeah, that is."

"Don't judge; you kill people," Darrel replied.

Once I heard the words come out of his mouth, it finally hit me that I was a murderer. Sasha wanted revenge from anyone I had gotten close to.

"Hey, it was really nice talking to you, but I have to go," I told Darrel.

"Where are you going? I'll come with you."

"No its okay I can manage."

"Nope, I'm not leaving you alone. We're friends now," he stated.

"Come on I'm going to watch a movie in the showroom."

Darrel got up from the table and followed me to the showroom. All of the sofas in the good spots were all taken. We had to settle for the old one in the back. I didn't want to be on that love seat with him because he was extremely attractive, and he could read me like an open book. There was something about him, and I just couldn't put a pin on it yet.

Chapter 8

June 3, 2013, I felt weak, tired, scared, and homesick. I thought I was going to die. I just wanted to stay in my bed and not leave. As I was thinking about going back to sleep, Darrel was knocking on my door being extra annoying like always. He never let me be alone unless I was taking a shower, using the bathroom, or sleeping. But he was sure to be outside of the door whenever he had the chance. I was starting to think he was weird; I'm not buying the story of him lighting things on fire. It can't be; it just can't. I got up from my bed and walked over to the door. When I opened it, there he was holding two notebooks and pens in his hands.

"Hey, what's up?"

"Nothing, let's go get breakfast."

"I'm not really hungry, and I just want to be left alone."

"Are you sure Janelle?"

"Yes, thanks for asking. I'll find you later."

I closed the door and laid back in the bed. Since I hadn't seen Blake in a few weeks due to him being away for work and being tired all of the time, I felt like we were falling apart. I really needed to see him and my son. I wanted to hold my son so bad. It was frustrating that I hadn't even been able to hold him or even be a mother. In mid thought, I could hear someone banging on the door. I thought it was Darryl and didn't want to open it.

"Janelle? It's me, Doctor Landry; can I come in?"

I sat up in the bed and made sure my nipples weren't hard since I wasn't wearing a bra and it was literally below zero in my room. I didn't know why they said that was the best psychiatric office to be in when they couldn't even make sure it was at least 60 degrees in everyone's room.

"Yes come in."

"Hey Janelle, how's everything going?"

"Everything's going well. I would love to leave this place and go back to my family."

Doctor Laundry started to chuckle. I wanted to know what he thought was so funny. If it was that he thought I would never leave, then I was going to kill myself.

"It's funny that you mentioned that because that's exactly what I came here to talk to you about."

"Really?"

I sat up a little more hoping he was about to tell me that Blake wasn't away for work and that he was in the lobby waiting for me to come out. I wanted him to tell me to throw out those tired old clothes and walk out to my family. I needed him to say that was going to be the best day of my life, that there wasn't anything wrong with me. I wanted to wake up in my bed and see that all of this was nothing but a horrible nightmare.

"Yes. Since you've been here for a while and you haven't acted out other than when you told me that you killed your...."

Doctor Landry looked down before he could say another word.

"It's ok Doctor Landry; I've gotten over it since I've made friends with Darrel a few weeks ago. He's really helped me cope with it, and now it's just a lot easier to talk about."

"Well, that's good Janelle. I'm so proud of you!"

"Thanks."

"Can I ask you a question?" I continued.

"Shoot."

"Well, since I did commit a crime when I was younger, when will I be doing my time? I need to say goodbye to my family at least."

I got up and walked over to my desk and picked up the pictures of Junior and Blake and started crying.

"Janelle, you never have to do time because no one but the people you told know what you have done. Since you weren't in the right mind and have a mental disorder, they cannot hold it against you. But if I did think you weren't able to live a somewhat normal life, I wouldn't be letting you out a lot earlier than we expected."

"Really? So I guess I am not as crazy as everyone has been making me feel.'' Doctor Landry and I both started laughing.

"Nope, and we have been keeping a close watch on you anyway. And between you and I, Darrel isn't really crazy. He's a doctor that we use to talk to the patients to see how they react around him. You were the only person who actually took the time to try and figure him out and became friends with him.''

"I knew something was off with him; I didn't buy that whole fire burning story he had told me when we first met. So Doctor Landry, when am I able to leave this place? I am so ready."

"You can leave in a few more months under a few circumstances."

"I knew there was a catch, but I'll do anything to get out of here."

"We will discuss that next week. Okay?''

"Okay."

"Enjoy the rest of your day. Go find Darrel and tell him his secret is out." Doctor Landry smiled, got up and reached in for a hug. When we hugged, I was trying not to hug him so close since my nipples were rock hard, but he was so damn friendly. He gave me a bear hug, and I felt him tense up when he felt my breast up against his chest. He backed up and smiled.

"I'll go turn on the heat for you."

He walked away with the biggest smile on his face. I got up to put on the white V-neck t-shirt, dark blue jeans, and my black Converse that I was only able to wear since they didn't want us wearing too much color or other shoes. It was around 7:45 p.m. and the cooks were preparing dinner; I had to wait until 8 to eat, so I decided to go and look for Darrel. I needed to tell someone the good news about being able to leave soon. I couldn't believe I would be able to see my son soon; I wanted to hold him so bad. It hurt me every day that he didn't even know who I was but going home was the most important thing in my life at that moment. I didn't know where Darrel would be, sometimes he was hanging out with other patients, and when he wasn't doing that, we were together. I figured I would find him later on during the day messing with these patients, so I decided to just head up to the movie room upstairs. It was one of my favorite places because it was one of the quietest areas on the second floor when it wasn't packed. I usually spent a lot of time up there.

There were only a few people in the room; they were watching the end of Avatar. I made my way over to one of the sofas in the back but remembered that I didn't have my blanket with me. I decided to walk back to my room to get it and hopefully I would see Darrel downstairs. As I was walking back out of the room, one of the older nurses announced that the movie was about to be over in 15 minutes and whoever could not be in the movie room had to leave, which were the few people in there watching Avatar. Usually, around dinner time everyone left, and we weren't under any supervision during that time, but most of the people who needed to be supervised had to get permission to even be on the second floor.

It was about to be dinner time, and they needed to be downstairs in the café before the third bell.

I was walking down the west wing to get to my room when I didn't see Darrel anywhere. It was awkward not seeing him roaming the halls or even talking to me. I would usually see him bothering someone throughout the day, and at this time I didn't notice him anywhere. Once I got to my room, I changed my pants and put on a pair of shorts and my slippers. I took my shoulder length curly blonde hair out of the bun. I massaged my head for a few seconds and left the hair tie on the night table by my bed. Before I left, I looked in the mirror and noticed that my roots were not black but dark brown. I knew it was time to go because my hair had grown 5 inches. My natural hair was a dark brown color, which I believe I inherited from my great- grandfather. My hair had grown so much since I'd been there with all of the vitamins and pills they had me taking daily. I forgot what I even looked like with brown hair since I hadn't kept it brown in a few years. I thought maybe I would dye my hair brown or something once I got home. I needed a change, and I didn't know if that would happen once I got home, so maybe dying my hair would make me feel better. I didn't want to cut it. I loved how my curls fell on my shoulders and how bouncy they were before arriving at the mental hospital. They had become extremely dry and brittle.

As I was walking back to the movie room, I hoped I would see Darrel on my way there because I didn't want to be alone. Well, I actually wanted his company. I liked being around him because we got along very well. If I wasn't been married, then he would have been my type, and I would have made love to him all night.

Wait. What was I talking about? I was married and happy. I needed to stop thinking about him like that. I always seemed to take the longest way to the movie room. When I was alone, I took the stairs to the second floor instead of the elevator whenever I had to get there. I did most of my thinking and crying during that walk. There was a painting on the wall that I looked at on my way upstairs. When I really took a good look at it, the author's name read, Darrel Turner. I couldn't believe he was an artist; I loved that painting.

Every time I looked at the painting, it made me think about my struggle and how I was overcoming it each and every day.

"Please make your way to the movie room; it is romantic night for the next two days. We will begin in two minutes," said the Asian lady who coordinated the night shows. By the time I made it up two flights of steps, I sat on the sofa in the back of the room and noticed that only a few people were there as usual. No one cared for those movies like they loved the action films that played most of the week. I loved romantic movies; they were my second favorite genre next to comedy. I took my slippers off and laid across the sofa since I knew that I would be there all night watching movies by myself. I had gotten comfortable watching *Dear John.* After about 20 minutes, someone touched me on the foot, nudging me to move over. Since my face was hidden under my blanket, I couldn't see the individual. As I continued watching the movie, all of a sudden I felt a heavy body come crashing down on me, crushing my bones. "What the hell! You don't see all of the other empty seats?" I looked up and saw that it was Darryl and immediately smiled. I got up and hugged him so tight. It felt so good just being able to see him. He hugged me back, and when I realized that I was hugging him a little too tight, I let go and moved over for him to sit down.

"Hey, Sunshine. How are you?"

"I'm good. And yourself? Can you stay?"

"Yes, of course, I can, move over. And by the way, I'm fine now that I'm here with you." He smiled and gave me a kiss on the cheek. I didn't know If he remembered that I was married or if he was just being nice since we were friends, but I didn't say anything about it because I didn't want to assume anything. We finished watching *Dear John* and waited for the next movie to play when we realized that we were the only two people left in the room. It was a quarter to eight, and we made our way to the dining room to eat dinner.

"Don't you love romantic movies, Janelle?" Darryl asked.

"Yes I do, they're my favorite. I would watch them every day if I could."

"I know what you mean, most of the time that's what me and my girlfriend used to do. We would spend a whole watching romantic movies on the weekend."

"That's so cute, Blake and I would spend Sundays and watch any independent movie we could find and pig out on ice cream and his favorite junk foods. We would be so sick by the third movie, fall asleep on the couch, and get up late on Monday mornings." Just the thought of doing that made me smile. I missed Blake so much.

"What do you want for dinner?"

"Steak and potatoes please."

"Okay, I'll be right back? Take a seat. I'll go and get it." As I looked around, there weren't any empty tables, so I walked to the line where Darryl was waiting.

"Hey. No tables?"

"Nope, we could go back up to the movie room."

"Ditto," said Darryl. I walked to the entrance of the café to wait for him when Joanna came over just to be nosey and ask me if I had seen her mom. I felt bad for her because she was really out of it at times, and I wished I could help her.

"Hey Nelly, I see you and that guy all of the time. I am watching you guys; you are so cute together. Are you'll dating because I could perform your wedding any day. Like I said before, I am just waiting for my license to officiate weddings to arrive in the mail."

"No it's okay Jo, we are just friends, and plus I am already married."

"But you guys like each other, I can tell "

"Oh hey Jo, how are you? Do you want to join us for dinner in the movie room?" Darryl asked.

"No, thank you, I have to find my mom." She smiled and winked at me.

"Okay, see you later Jo."

"Okay Nelly, see you later."

"What was that about?" Darryl asked curiously.

"What?" I replied.

"The wink?" Darryl started smiling.

"Stop smiling, she thinks we are dating and that we look good together. Crazy right?" I looked away not wanting to know what he was going to say.

"No, it's not crazy. Everyone's been asking me if we are a couple or if I have fallen for the crazy girl."

"What? I am not crazy, well not that crazy." I responded.

"It's okay; we all are."

"No we all aren't because I know your secret. Doctor Landry told me that you aren't really like anyone of us and that your just here to test everyone's actions, to see if our other personality will come out and react."

"Wow, he told you all of that? He really can't hold water to save his life." We both started laughing. We got to the elevator, and that's when it started to hit me. We both were silent, and I felt myself craving for any man's touch. I really missed being touched, being pleased, or even pleasing someone else. I was growing impatient waiting to leave and be with my husband again. I knew it was wrong to even think about him like that, but I knew he felt it as well because when I looked at him, he was staring at me. We both were adults and knew how to have self-control. When Darryl broke the tension, and we both realized that we never pressed the elevator button. He spoke first.

"Push the button, Janelle."

"Oh I'm sorry, I don't know what I was thinking about; I was really thinking about something."

"Yeah me too." We both got off of the elevator and walked into the movie room and sat on the sofa where we were earlier and began to eat.

After we both had finished eating, no one had come back up to the movie room, so we put on another movie.

"Oh my god, guess what."

"What?"

"Come on. Guess!"

"Are you pregnant?"

"Darryl that is impossible because I've been in here for five months, eleven days, thirty-four minutes, and about three seconds."

"Are you really keeping count?"

"Yes because I have nothing else better to do and plus I miss having sex, I enjoyed having sex with my husband." Just thinking about my husband turned me on. I didn't know if Darrel was staring at me because by then I was laying down facing the television.

"I enjoyed sex too, my girlfriend was such a tease, and she made a commitment that she wasn't going to have sex with me until

102

we got married. I was not trying to marry her until after we have been together for a while, so we ended it."

"So you just ended it because she didn't want to have sex with you?"

"Yes, a brother was not trying to wait years.''

"That's selfish as hell Darryl."

"Shit she was being selfish too."

Chapter 9

I woke up wrapped in Darrel's arms lying on the sofa in the movie room. I felt uncomfortable being held by someone other than my husband. I jumped up from the couch, put on my slippers, and headed back to my room. When I got in, I looked at the clock. It read 6:36 a.m. I climbed into my bed, took off my bra, and started reading one of Zane's books that my husband sent me. Reading that novel made me realize that I almost took advantage of my somewhat freedom by spending the night with a guy that I found mentally, physically, and sexually attractive. I was trying to remember how I ended up in his arms under the same blanket and even being able to get up so quickly without waking him. The last thing I remember was us eating dinner and talking about our sex lives. After that, I didn't recall anything else. He must've drugged me.

"Janelle shut up; that man did not drug you."

Okay, now I'm talking to myself and confused as hell. I was thinking about what Doctor Landry needed me to do to stay sane until I went home to live a normal life. Who was I kidding though; my life would never be normal if Sasha continued to live in my head. She seemed to only come out or take over when she wanted to kill someone close to me. I hated my condition, but I would never wish it on anyone. You have no control over anything that happens once the other side of you takes over. I drifted off to sleep and got up around 10:15 with Blake sitting on the chair near the window in my room.

"Blake?"

"Yes, it's me babe."

"Oh my god, what are you doing here?"

"Well, Doctor Landry needed to talk to me about you, and I came to see if you were awake, but you weren't, so I watched you sleep for an hour."

"That's not normal; you could have just woke me up."

"I know, but I wanted you to rest."

"Thanks. But come over here and hug me. I've missed you so much."

Blake got up and walked over to my bed and wrapped his arms around me. Feeling his warmth on my body seemed to warm me and made me relax. Just having a familiar but not so familiar person touch me, felt good. Being in Blake's arms made me realize that Darryl had nothing on him, he was my husband, someone I gave my all to, my child's father. Nothing or no one could ever replace him. I loved Blake not only for him being my husband but for him sticking out and riding with me during this journey.

"I love you, baby."

"I love you too, Janelle."

"Did you talk to Doctor Landry yet?"

"No, why?"

"Because he said that I would be able to leave soon but under a few circumstances. He said he wouldn't send me to jail for the crimes I committed because I wasn't in the right mind. However, if I commit more murders, then I will probably be locked in here for the rest of my life. And that scares me so much. I don't want to be known as your crazy wife or Junior's crazy, unfit mother."

"Janelle relax, no one will be saying any of that." I looked away and got back under my blanket.

"Look at me. Listen, you have to speak positive things into existence because the more you put yourself down the more you will defeat yourself. Do you think I was always positive about our situation for the past five months, no I wasn't. There were days when I felt like I needed to leave you here and not look back; I wanted to put our son in a foster home because I was having a hard time dealing with being a single father. I needed my wife at home, taking care of the both of us. I needed to have sex with my wife. I needed to hold you, here your voice, and eat your cooking. Most of all, I wanted our son to get to know his mother, not just me and his babysitter. It was hard most of the time, but baby I had to keep faith alive and think about how you were going to get better and come home to us."

"I'm sorry babe; I didn't realize how this was really affecting you. I love you."

"Don't apologize, you have nothing to be sorry for; it's not like you planned to be crazy." Blake smiled and wiped the tears off of my face.

"Thank you for sticking through this ride out with me. I cannot wait until I can go home and finally go back to my life. I miss being able to go shopping." We both started laughing.

"You're crazy. But go get ready so we can go meet with Doctor Landry. I got up from my bed, grabbed the only clothes we were able to wear, and headed for the shower.

"Hey Janelle, wake up?"

As I waited for Janelle, I heard someone calling for her to wake up. Then I heard a knock on the door.

"I'm sorry, I thought Janelle was here, but you must be Blake her husband. She talks about you all the time. I'm Darrel."

"What's up? How are you?"

"I'm good, well since she's not here, I'll come back later. Nice meeting you."

"Wait; can you tell me how my wife is doing?"

"Sure. She's doing really well, she's actually really sane, and she's the normal one in the bunch."

"Are you sure? I know you're just like her, but are you one hundred percent sure she's doing okay. Is she capable of doing basic activities?"

"Yes, she is and by the way, I am a doctor. I am a fake; I am here to monitor the rest of them here, and I analyze their actions when new people come up to them. I tend to fool the mind and get them going just to see if they can control the other side. Your wife might have multiple personality disorder, but she is far from crazy. I just think she needs a little more TLC at home, and she should be fine. She may need a little counseling here and there, but she will do well as long as she keeps taking the meds they prescribe to her."

"How do I know you know what you are talking about? I don't really know who you are or even what you do for a living. For all I know, you could be the janitor."

"Trust me I am no janitor, and I make way more money than a janitor. I am actually a doctor, a psychologist to be exact. I used to work here with Doctor Landry."

"Thank you, thank you for letting me know how she's doing. I appreciate it."

"No problem, but let me get back to work. Tell Janelle I stopped by."

"Sure I will," said Blake.

Chapter 10

Blake

Talking to that guy definitely made it a lot easier on me. I felt a lot more confident in my wife. It had been a long ride, but it was all worth it. I was praying she wouldn't try to kill us again. I just wanted to move forward instead of backward. As I was waiting for Janelle to get out of the shower, I began to think about how he had taken the time to get to know my wife. He knew her more than I did. I didn't know that side of her. I was getting a bad vibe, but I didn't want to assume anything because I knew my wife would never cheat on me.

"Hey babe."

"Are you ready?"

Janelle looked beautiful; I forgot how good she looked when she took the time to get ready. I hadn't seen my wife like that in so long. I had forgotten. She had slimmed down since the baby but also gained weight in places I didn't know were capable of getting bigger. She definitely looked gorgeous. The light blue jeans and white tank top fit her so well. She had on a black sweater. She always wore bigger tops. To see her in a tight one made me fall in love with her new body. She was stunning. Her hair was out of the twists she had earlier, and it had grown so much. My wife looked like a brand new woman. She still looked like the old Janelle. She still acted like Janelle, but the only thing different was her outer appearance.

"You look beautiful baby."

"Thank you. You don't think I gained a little too much weight in my hips and butt?"

"No, you look perfect."

"Thanks." She came over and kissed me, and I had to restrain myself from throwing her on the bed.

"Are you ready to go and talk to Doctor Landry?"

"Yes, but can we first just stay in each other's company for about an hour?"

"Yes, anything for you."

"Let's go watch a movie; I just want to cuddle."

"Me too Janelle, cuddle that booty."

I started laughing. Janelle slapped me on the arm. I pushed her on the bed. She hit the bed so hard; I thought the picture on the wall would fall.

"Blake really? Are you trying to kill me before I get to leave?" she said smiling.

"Sorry babe," I said laughing. Janelle tried to get up off the bed when I jumped on top of her, holding her down.

"You're crushing me, oh my god get off of me."

"Janelle, why are you being dramatic; you know I am not crushing you."

"Yes you are, I'm losing air as we speak."

"Okay, I'll get off of you."

I was getting up when she pulled me back down. I loved this. We were enjoying each other's company. I only wished our son was here laughing and enjoying our family time.

"I thought you wanted me to get up?" I asked smiling.

"No, not for real. I'm enjoying this."

Chapter 11

After cuddling for an hour, we finally got up and made our way to Doctor Landry's office. It couldn't have felt more comfortable, but we both knew we would have to go our separate ways at the end of the meeting. We both knew I couldn't come home, and we couldn't make love to each other yet. It broke my heart that I had to let him leave me another day. We weren't going to see each other for a few more weeks, and I thought it was going to be the death of me. I was growing tired of not going home to my family. Walking the halls of Sweet Hollow Homes, I noticed that I really didn't belong there. My time was way far spent. The place had become more hectic. Everyone was always in their rooms screaming, crying, yelling, or fighting a nurse. I hated it. I didn't know if it was because I wanted to leave so bad. I came to realize that it wasn't a home for anyone.

"Blake, do you think I am crazy?"

"No, well not anymore since I've talked to Darrel."

"When did you talk to him?"

"He came in to see you, but you were in the shower?"

"Really? What did he say that changed your mind?"

"He said that you didn't belong in here, and he didn't think that you were as bad as the rest of the people in here. He also said that you're not out of your mind but just have some type of multiple personality disorder."

"Like there is a difference."

"Walking down these halls make me think that there is a difference."

"I hope so." By the time we reached Doctor Landry's office, he was already waiting for us.

"Hey, guys come on in. Don't you two look like a couple in love." He grinned.

"Yes, we are happily in love," said Blake. I just smiled.

"Okay, so let's talk about letting Janelle leave soon. Take a seat," said Doctor Landry.

We both sat down next to each other awaiting the news from the doctor. Blake grabbed my hand. As much as I wanted to let go because I needed to rub my leg, I kept my hand in his. I started to rub my other leg as Doctor Landry began telling us the good news.

"Well, as you both already know, I think it's about time that Janelle goes back to her regular life. She is capable of living life outside of here as long as she keeps taking her medication, attends counseling once a week, and whenever she feels like things are not getting better, she will come here or call Darrell. If she cannot follow those rules, then it's back in here, and we will continue to run more tests. Now can you follow these few rules?"

"Of course I can. I will follow all of them."

"Good."

"When will she be able to come home?" asked Blake.

117

"She is able to leave today if that is okay with you guys. I know I said in a few months, but I believe in her, and I know she will be just fine."

I jumped up off of the couch and ran out of the office. I didn't know where I was headed, but I had to get out of that building. The only thing I heard was, "You can go home today." Then I ran out of the office and straight into Darrel.

"Oh my god, I'm so sorry. I didn't mean to run into you like that."

"It's okay Janelle, why are you so excited?"

"I get to go home today."

"I can see that. I'm so proud of you. Don't forget me now."

"Oh I won't forget you, and plus were friends. I can't forget my only sane friend in here."

"Oh wow, your only sane friend. Thanks, I feel special."

"You are special. Thank you for listening to me and keeping me on my toes."

"No problem, I enjoyed spending time with such a beautiful, intelligent young lady."

"Thanks, I'll keep in touch. If I ever feel like I'm falling apart, Doctor Landry instructed me to call you or him."

"Oh great, that's good. Here, take my card. Call me anytime, even if it's just to talk or to hook me up with one of your beautiful friends."

"Oh yes, I might have the perfect girl for you."

"If she's anything like you, I'll love her automatically. But let me get going. See you soon."

"Okay bye."

What did he mean "if she's anything like you, I will automatically love her?" He knows that I'm married. If I made him think any other way, I really need to let him know I didn't mean that.

"Janelle?" I turned around and noticed Blake calling me from the end of the hallway.

"Yes? What's up?"

"Nothing, but damn baby, you ran out of there so quick. You didn't even get to say bye to Doctor Landry."

"I know. I'll go back and say goodbye, but I was so excited."

"I know you were, you jumped over me and ran out of the office. Let's go pack up your room."

"Alright."

Going into my room to pack everything up to go home was a little bittersweet; I wasn't going to see Darryl every day anymore, nor would I get to enjoy free movies. I used to think I would never leave, but I was actually going to leave before my son turned one. I would be able to build a bond and love him. I could finally watch him grow up. I hadn't seen pictures of him in a while; I wondered if he looked more like me now than his father. I wanted to know if he was right handed or left handed, if he was speaking yet, or if he still had that birthmark around his eye. I needed to know if my baby even knew who I was, if he would scream Mommy when I walked through the door, or if he remembered me from our only meet and greet.

"Okay? Are you ready?"

"Yes, I think so." We started to get out of the car to pick up junior when I realized I shouldn't be walking into the babysitter's house. I felt weird going to meet her when it was her last day.

"Wait babe, can I just wait in the car? You go ahead and get him."

"Alright, I'll be right back." he turned the car back on and squeezed my hand.

"I love you." He walked up to the babysitter's house and went inside. I was so nervous waiting for Blake to bring Junior to the car. I didn't want to see him, and he didn't remember me or think I was his mother. I wished I had my phone so that I could call someone. I wished Jean was still alive, I wished he wasn't murdered, and I hated feeling like that was my fault as well. After about 15 minutes, Blake came out carrying Junior in his hands. Junior had the biggest smile on his face. He was grinning from ear to ear. I couldn't help but smile. I got out of the car and ran up to them. I looked at Junior for a few seconds. I reached out, and he jumped into my arms hugging me. He was hugging me so tight that I thought he was going to suffocate me. I turned around and walked to the car; Blake opened the car door. As I was strapping Junior in his car seat, I wanted to cry. I'd been dreaming about that moment for months. Finally being able to do it made me feel emotional. I never thought I was going to leave that hospital or see my son. I was so blessed and grateful to get that opportunity.

Chapter 12

I woke up the next morning forgetting that I was home; I jumped up from the bed and looked around. I looked down next to me and Blake was still sleeping. I looked on the nightstand; it read 5:45 am. I got up from the bed and started to clean the house. It wasn't completely dirty, but it did smell like it hadn't had chemicals used on it for a few months. I could tell that Blake had done his best. I went into the kitchen to see if there was anything to eat when I noticed that there were a bunch of papers lying on the kitchen table. Being that some of the mail had my name on them, I looked through them. There were a few letters that I had written Blake in the pile and some bills. Then I came across a letter from the detective that was handling Jean's case. I grabbed it and walked over to the dining room table and began reading it. The detective was explaining that they didn't have a suspect, and they had worked diligently on his case but couldn't pinpoint the killer. They didn't have any evidence

123

or witnesses that could help them. I was reading the rest of the letter and started to cry because I knew deep down that I had killed my brother. I didn't know if I should turn myself in or not say anything. That had been bothering me since the first time I found out that I was the cause of my parent's death. It broke my heart knowing that I had murdered them, and it hurt me even more knowing that I could have killed my own brother. While heading back up to my bedroom, I went in to check on junior; he was still asleep. He was sleeping so peacefully; he slept on his stomach like his father and would take up the whole entire bed if he could. I watched him sleep for a few more minutes until Blake came up behind me scaring me half to death. I jumped and swore I had stopped breathing.

"Damn babe, I didn't mean to scare you like that."

"It's okay." I turned around to give him a kiss when he picked me up and carried me into the bedroom. He lay me on the bed and shut the door. He came over, leaned in for a kiss, and I immediately felt uncomfortable, which was weird because he's my husband and having sex with him should have been normal, but at that moment, I didn't know if I could have sex with him.

"Blake, wait."

"What's the matter, Janelle?"

"This doesn't feel awkward?"

"No, not really. You're my wife."

"I know, I guess it's just me." We kissed again.

The whole time we were having sex, I thought about how long it had been, how uncomfortable I felt, and how many times we made love that morning before Blake had enough. We used to have sex twice a night, but today I just wanted him to get off of me. Once it was over, I felt kind of disgusted and didn't want him to see me naked, so I stayed in bed and let him shower first. As I was lying there, I thought about how I was going to be a stay at home mom for a while. I didn't know what I was going to do with myself. I thought about becoming that mom who spends her whole day cleaning the house, preparing dinner, and going shopping. I really didn't want to stay at home, but due to my condition, I decided just to leave it alone and face the fact that no one was going to want to hire me if they knew why I had been out of work for so long. If I did get hired somewhere, would they treat me like I was incompetent? I would never move up or even do anything I really wanted to do. It would be like working retail all over again. The last time I worked a retail job, I was twenty-one, going to college, and didn't have any real bills to pay. Working a retail job now would be crazy as hell, it wouldn't even help me buy food for the house let alone help Blake pay any of the bills. Don't get me wrong, Blake gets paid well enough to pay every single bill in both of our names, but I just hated that I was not going to be working and doing what I loved. I remember the days when my parents couldn't get me to work. I hated working fast food and retail. I was always calling out or quitting after six months. I was the teenager who didn't mind having mommy and daddy support me. My parents spoiled Jean and I. They would have given us their last if we needed it. That's what I loved most about them. They never let us go without anything. We got every game system we wanted, toys, and phones My parents never made us think we were poor or even middle class. Growing up, I believed that we were the only rich black kids in the neighborhood until I reached high school. We were actually not even considered middle class, and we still held our heads high and made it day after day.

In the middle of my trip down memory lane, I received a call from my cousin Autumn. I was so excited to hear from her. I hadn't spoken to her since I went into labor. I didn't know if she was aware of my situation, but I didn't care because she was my best friend.

"Omg Autumn! Hi!" I said with excitement.

"Hi Nelly, how are you? I heard what happened. Blake just told me that you were finally home."

"I'm fine, just hate being home all day but, I'm fine."

"That's good. I miss you girl; we have to get together soon."

"I know we do. I have so much to tell you."

"No, I have so much to tell you."

"What are you doing tomorrow?"

"Nothing, I'm actually off tomorrow."

"Come over, and we can catch up."

"Okay definitely. I'll stop by around noon."

"Okay girl; I love you."

"I love you too Nelly."

Blake had left for work, and Junior was with his sister Rebecca. She was so beautiful; she had a short blonde pixie cut, really pale skin, long legs, and a really flattering body. She was stunning. When I first met her, we clicked right away. We were actually friends before Blake and I started dating. She was one of my few friends in high school, but we had parted a few years back when she moved to Japan for the military. She finally got out and decided to follow her dreams of becoming a nurse. I knew she wasn't comfortable with me being home alone with my son due to my condition, and it did bother me because I wouldn't purposely hurt anyone. Ever since I had returned home from the hospital, I felt like everyone was judging me and wouldn't let me just live. I felt like people were looking at me weird. I even noticed that Blake had hid most of our knives and his tools. It wasn't like I didn't expect it. However, when those that I love were more afraid of me than the people that were not family, it drove me insane. Everyone was worried about living than trying to help me get better. The last few days had been stressing me out, and it killed me that I hadn't been really communicating with anyone.

I decided to watch TV since the house was finally clean. Junior was with his aunt, and Blake was at work. Having the house to myself was pretty boring since I was used to being around a bunch of people running around like a maniac six days a week. I missed working five to six days, coming home to my husband, sleeping in late on Sundays, and enjoying him cook for us every other day. Since arriving home, I had been clearing, cooking, and sleeping. It was getting pretty old. I hated not doing anything productive. I flipped through the channels, looking to see if there were any good lifetime movies on until I came across the cooking channel and started watching six teams challenge each other. They had to make a cake based on a Disney movie. I was so into it that I didn't even realize that I had fallen asleep. I dreamed about my brother's death. I walked into the house and looked to see if my grandparents were home, which they weren't because they had gone to a hotel that night to celebrate their 50th wedding anniversary. As I walked into the basement, Jean was lying in the bed sleeping. He was wearing shorts and a t-shirt. He was knocked out. I called his name three times before I smashed the baseball bat into his ribs. He woke up and screamed in agony looking at me like I was crazy. He didn't know who it was hitting him, but he knew it was a female. Jean grabbed the bat and tried pulling it out of my hands. I was not letting go for the life of me. I ended up kicking Jean in the leg, and he let go. He got up off of the bed and tackled me to the ground. He was trying to win the fight when I grabbed him by his arm and squeezed it just enough to make him bleed. Jean grabbed me by my neck and forced me to the other side of the room, slamming me into the wall that had our family picture hanging on it. It was his wife's picture and the picture of our parents. Jean was very family oriented. After he had slammed me against the wall, I fell down searching for an object to throw at him because I didn't want to shoot him yet. As he was kicking me, I grabbed him by his legs and shoved him to the floor. I got on top of him, punching as hard as I could, making his lip bleed. I made sure my face was covered well so that I wouldn't get any bruises or scratches, but Jean punched me so hard in the mouth that I felt it swell up. I got up off of him and started running up the stairs so that he would follow me outside. I ended up tripping on the steps, and Jean was running after me. I heard him calling someone, and I turned around, took my gun out, and shot him in the arm. I tried to aim at his chest, but I missed. I got up off the floor and started searching the kitchen for knives when Jean hit me in the head. I fell to the floor; I was unconscious for a few seconds then I got back up and saw that Jean was on the phone calling my grandmother. As I got up off of the floor running and screaming that

I hated him, he was in defense mode and grabbed me. He yanked the gun out of my hands and pulled the mask off of my face. Jean noticed that it was me; he called out my name so loud that I had no choice but to kill him. I didn't want to go to jail for attempted murder, so I tried pushing him away and just running out of the house all the way home. I knew if I didn't kill him, he would have trapped me inside of the house. I tried so hard getting loose from his grip, I ran into the kitchen, grabbed a knife, and when I turned around, he was standing there trying to fight me. I stabbed him in the chest. I had stabbed him a total of six times when I noticed that he wasn't getting up off of the floor. I quickly ran to grab my gun. When I got back upstairs, I saw that he was outside on the lawn trying to escape when I shot him twice. The first time I shot him in the back, and the next time I aimed for his head but ended up missing and hit him in the neck. I didn't even stop to see if he was dead. I ran down the street to my car. I hopped in the driver's seat and started driving to get to the highway when I noticed that I had never changed my clothes. I stopped the car, changed my clothes, and dumped them over the bridge on my way home. I quickly made my way home. I got to my house, back into bed, and fell asleep.

I woke up from my nap confused as hell. I got up looking for my phone to call Blake when the clock on it said 6 p.m. I knew Blake was still at work. He didn't answer but texted me that he was in his last meeting and would be home around 6:45 p.m. I texted him back saying "I love you; I need you to come home." I didn't wait for him to respond. I started calling Darryl. I called him because I needed to know if my mind was making up this dream or if that was what really had happened, and I just remembered it. When Darryl picked up, I told him that I need a session ASAP. We made the appointment for the next afternoon, and I couldn't wait.

Chapter 13

Waking up to my husband and child on a Tuesday morning was the highlight of the beginning of the week. Blake was half carrying Junior and carrying the breakfast that he had made. He was an excellent cook. God bless his mother because she had taught him well. I loved when he made dinner because he wouldn't just cook Creole dishes but would cook anything from the millions of cookbooks we had lined up on the kitchen counter. Most of the counter were lined up full of his mother's recipes or cookbooks he had over time. Blake knew that food was my first love when we met. When we ran into each other for the second time, I was at dinner with my girls and was the only one who ordered most of the food at the table. He came up to the table as I was stuffing my face. He walked over, and my friend Bianca thought he was hitting on her. She was smiling so hard, and I was sitting next to her laughing. She even nudged me to stop. Blake reached past her and put his hand out

134

to grab mine. He made a stupid comment like, "That's all for you, or you sure can eat." I remember just sitting there smiling because he wasn't supposed to know how I got down before we actually went out on a date. I felt so embarrassed.

"Babe this is so sweet. Thank you." Blake placed the TV tray on my lap and put Junior down. Then Junior crawled over and tried to take the bacon off of my plate.

"Junior, wait." He got mad and threw the bacon back onto my plate. From that point on, I knew he had my temper.

"Boy, you better act right." yelled Blake.

"Here, Junior." I gave him some eggs and started eating myself. Blake got into bed and lay down on the other side. He began grabbing food off of my plate as well.

"I thought you made breakfast for me?"

"I did. For you, but for you to share."

"Babe that makes no sense."

"I know. Let me get that piece of sausage right there." He reached over and grabbed the sausage, and I grabbed him by the ear and gave him a kiss.

"Baby I love you, and I am so thankful to have you in my life."

"Janelle that's what a husband is supposed to do. I do it because I want to not because I have too. Give me another kiss; you taste like bacon." We both started laughing, and in the middle, junior started cracking up with us. It was so cute. He was watching us the whole time. Then once we started laughing, he threw himself down laughing. We couldn't help but to crack up even more. We definitely had a good family moment. I lived for those moments.

After we had finished eating breakfast, I got up and jumped in the shower; I was finally about to leave the house, so the shower I took was well worth it. Blake was in the bedroom, and Junior was in his room playing in his play pin. I'd been doing nothing but thinking about how my disease was affecting me mentally, and how it might be affecting my family, well mostly my husband. That was a

136

constant struggle. I got out of the shower and saw that Blake had fallen back to sleep and was letting the news watch him. He must have been exhausted from working late the past few weeks. I didn't want to wake him, so I got dressed quickly. I put on a black romper and black sandals. I took my hair out of the bun and added some water and conditioner to it. I didn't feel like putting on makeup except for my usual eyeliner and mascara. I grabbed my wallet and car keys off of the dresser. I walked over to the nightstand and wrote a note saying where Junior and I were going. I went into Junior's room, and he was sleeping as well. I had a house full of lazy men. Since he was asleep and dressed, I didn't want to wake him to give him a bath, so I picked him up and headed out of the door. I was strapping Junior in his car seat when I noticed Blake standing in the front door looking at me.

"Where are you going?"

"Blake I told you last night that I had an appointment with Darryl today."

"No, you didn't."

"Blake I told you that when you got home and after we talked about the dream I had."

"No, you did not, why are you lying?"

"I am not lying. What exactly are you mad about?"

"Janelle, get in the house; you are not going anywhere."

"What is wrong with you? I am not your child."

"No, but you're my wife."

"Exactly, I am your wife. So why are you now trying to be the boss."

"Janelle, don't test me, just get in the house. You are not going anywhere." I finished strapping Junior in his seat, and I hopped into the car. Blake saw me and started running towards it. I put the key in the ignition and started the engine. I pulled off as Blake was pulling and banging on the door, telling me to stop the car. I didn't know why he was bugging out and not wanting me to see Darryl. That was the first time that he acted strangely. Since I had been home, he had been cool. It was actually scary because he never showed this much anger other than when we argued, but today it was different; He was controlling. I got onto the highway and ended up calling Darryl to let him know that I had to cancel the meeting and would explain it if he could meet me for lunch. I was so glad that he agreed because I didn't want to go back to the house right away. As I was making my way downtown, I was getting a call from Autumn.

"Hey Autumn. Can you do me a favor?"

"Yes, sure Nelly. What's up? Aren't you coming over later?"

"No, there's a change of plans. I need to drop Junior off at your house for a few hours. I will explain once I pick him up. Blake might call you or come by your house. If he wants to take him, you can let him, but don't tell him where I am going."

"Nelly, what are you talking about? I need you to explain to me what's going on."

"Blake and I got into a fight. I need my space for a second. Can you watch Junior?"

"Yes, of course, I can, but why is it so dramatic this time?"

"I can't explain it right now. It's a long story."

"Okay, come on over. I'll be home. If he calls or stops by before you, I'll call you."

"Thank you girl. I love you."

My favorite song was on the radio; I had to turn it up and sing at the top of my lungs. I looked in the mirror to see if Junior was still sleeping and he was. He had slept through everything. I was making my way to Autumn's house when I got another call from Blake. I didn't want to pick up, so I ignored the seven missed calls.

"What?" I screamed.

"Where are you, Janelle?"

"Why? Does it matter?"

"Yes, it does. I want to know where you are taking my son."

"Our son."

"Where are you?"

"Dropping him off at his aunt's house while I go to this meeting. I will see you later at the house. I don't want to argue."

"Janelle, which aunt?"

"Figure it out. Goodbye." As I was hanging up, I heard Blake saying *I love you*. He was acting really strange, and I couldn't figure out why.

Junior was awake by the time we got to Autumn's apartment. He was smiling, hitting me with his truck, and biting his fingers. He had started teething; he was always in so much pain. When I reached her front door, I had to knock three times so that she would know it was me. Since we were kids, we always had a bunch of codes and nicknames for each other. We never let go of our childhood. Waiting for her to come to the door, I thought Blake would be there, but I also thought that maybe he wasn't going to come and find him. He knew I would never leave him where we both didn't trust the person, plus we both didn't have that much family out here anyway. Now that our parents were no longer living, we only had each other, other than my cousin and his sister. They were our only family besides my grandparents. I waited a few more seconds, and when I went to knock again, Autumn opened the door. She had a weird look on her face which made me aware that Blake had either been there or was still there.

"He's here?"

"No."

"Then what's the matter?"

"He will be here in a few minutes. You better hurry up girl."

"Okay, thanks. I went inside to sit Junior down and to leave money if she needed to get anything that I didn't pack. I sat Junior on the floor, and he started crawling all over the living room, chasing her dog Becca.

"Thanks again, I owe you."

"No, you don't. I love you, go ahead and leave before he shows up."

"Okay I left some money for you to order food and all of his bottles are in his bag, there's extra milk, diapers, wipes…"

"Girl I know, get going." I was walking out of Autumn's building when I received a call from Darryl.

"Hey, what's up?"

"Hey Janelle, meet me at the Panera Bread on Fulton Street downtown. I will be there waiting for you."

"Okay I'm actually right around the corner; I'll be there in a few minutes."

"Okay, see you then."

"Bye."

Making my way to the Panera down the street from Autumn's, I had to make sure I didn't end up running into Blake. It wasn't that I was avoiding him, but I didn't want to be bothered nor did I want to argue about something so petty. Blake was really making the day difficult, and I didn't like it. He was changing, and I didn't know how to respond. I couldn't figure out if he thought that I was going to murder someone or if I'd end up coming back to kill him or our son. I hated my condition.

Chapter 14

I had made a right on the corner of Washington and Adams when I saw Darryl sitting in the window of Panera. He was looking so good that I caught myself smiling. It was actually going to be a good lunch. Going out and spending time with someone other than my family was what I needed. Even though it was with a man my husband didn't want me talking to, I was still going to enjoy my day if I had to fake it. I parked the car and looked into the mirror to make sure the little bit of makeup I was wearing wasn't smudged. I put on some chapstick and fixed my hair. I got out of the car, grabbed my bag, and walked over to the building. I walked past the long line of people waiting to order their food and headed to the table where Darryl was sitting. Walking over to the table, I was getting excited; I was trying so hard not to smile, but once Darryl looked up at me, I couldn't help it. He was wearing a black short sleeve shirt, light blue jeans and a pair of Jordan's. I could tell by the way he was looking

145

at me that he was glad to see me. I walked little closer to the table, and he got up from where he was sitting and hugged me. He hugged me tight but not too tight, just enough for me to feel his heartbeat and feel comfortable.

"So how are you, Janelle?"

"I'm okay, not the strongest or the happiest, but I will make it."

"Have you been taking your medication? Have you been depressed lately?"

"Wow, okay. Um, I have been taking my medication but not as much as when I first got home. I'm just trying to get used to being home all day and having to take care of a family now. This is actually the first time I've been out with someone other than my family."

"Okay, well everything you're telling me sounds normal."

"Normal? Come on, my life has never been normal."

"At one point in your life, it had to have been normal. If not normal, then I like that about you." said Darryl smiling.

"Well enough about me, have you found that special someone yet?" I smiled.

"No, not yet, but I wish I did. I get so lonely sometimes. Going out with my boys are not as fun as it used to be. They all have wives or girlfriends now."

"I know what you mean. When I first got married my friends hated hanging out with me, most of them were single and didn't want any part of being in a relationship. But now they are looking for someone to marry."

"Janelle, didn't I say to hook me up with one of your friends?"

"Darryl, didn't you say that you wanted someone like me?"

"Yeah, I did, but I'm desperate now."

"I do have a cousin that you might like. She's cute."

147

"Cute? What's wrong with her if she's just cute?"

"Nothing is wrong with her; she's my cousin. I'm not going to make her sound beautiful until you see her for yourself. But just know if you guys date I'm going to be all up in your business."

"I respect that. Why did you want to meet today anyway? What is really going on?"

"To be honest, I had a dream about killing my brother. It felt so real, and when I woke up, I didn't know if maybe it was my mind replaying something it remembered or some kind of Déjà vu crap. I'm a little nervous because if that is the way I killed my brother I really won't be able to live with myself."

"I don't think you murdered your brother; I think you dreamt about it because it's been on your mind so much. I think your fine."

"Why do you keep saying that I am fine when I'm not?"

"Because I believe that nothing's wrong with you, Janelle, and I'm trying to figure you out. I deal with patients with personality disorders all day long, and you don't act anything like them. We

148

have been here for almost a half an hour, and you seem fine. You don't seem like you're hearing any voices; you haven't acted out in any way."

"So are you saying that you don't think that I have a mental disorder?"

"Yes, that is what I am saying. But I also don't know if you have a tad bit, and it is just being treated well with the medication."

"Darryl I love you, oh my God this is the best news that I have gotten in a long time."

"Janelle?"

"Wait. But how do you explain the killing of my brother?"

"Well, that I don't know. You will have to take some time to figure that out, or we can do it together."

"This is a lot to take in right now."

"I know, so let's change the subject. How's the family?"

"They're good. Junior is growing so much; he's looking more and more like his father."

"How's the husband?"

"Blake?" I looked out of the window and let the sun beam on my face until Darryl touched my hand. I quickly moved my hand away and looked him in the eyes.

"Are you hungry?"

"Yes, I thought you would never ask?"

We both got up to order something to eat. We got to the front of the store. The line wasn't as long as when I first got there. There were only three people in front of us. We waited in silence because I was thinking about what Darryl had said about me not actually sick or as bad as they thought. I couldn't wrap my finger around it, but I thought it was strange. How would they even keep me in a mental institution if nothing was wrong with me? How could they say that I told the truth about murdering my parents but also say that I never acted out or anything? Why did they say I was the normal one in the group? I didn't understand how that could even be true. I was starting to feel weak. I didn't know if it was because I was on my period and my iron was low. I hadn't been taking my iron pills. I also didn't know if it was because I was overwhelmed; I felt like I would pass out. I was on my phone checking my email when the cashier yelled for the next person in line. I walked up to the register and ordered a large cheddar and broccoli soup and a green tea. The lady was looking at me weird the whole time until I paid for my meal. I walked over to the side and waited for Darryl to finish ordering. I felt like the room was spinning. I bent down to lean on the counter because I was really dizzy. Darryl came over and put his hand on my back; he tried lifting me up off of the counter. When he tried picking my head up, I felt this heavy pressure. I needed to keep my head down.

"Darryl stop. I can't lift up. Wait a minute."

"Janelle, what's wrong with you?"

"I feel dizzy and weak. Just give me a few minutes." Darryl was rubbing my back softly while asking me a million and one questions. I heard one of the workers asking if they needed to call 911. I made Darryl tell them no because the dizziness started going away. I lifted my head off of the counter slowly, and he was still holding on to me.

"Janelle are you okay now? Are you still dizzy?"

"I'm not that dizzy anymore; I'm okay now."

"Are you sure? I can take you to the emergency room."

"No, that won't be necessary."

Darryl walked me back to the table and went back to get the food that we had ordered. My head was still bothering me, so I had decided to lay my head down on the table and wait for Darryl to come back. He was taking a long time with the food, so I decided to go and see what was going on. I got up from the chair and was headed to the food area when my legs started feeling weak, and everything started to fade. I closed my eyes, and as I went to open them back up and take another step, I fell onto the floor and knocked over the table that was on the side of me. I didn't remember waking up and going to the emergency room or how I had gotten into the ambulance. I woke up in the hospital room with IV's in my hand and Blake sitting next to the window. He was on his phone doing something, and he didn't even notice that I was awake. I lay there for a while and thought about Darryl and where he had gone, who had called Blake and how he reacted when he found out where I was. I was still a little uneasy about what Darryl had told me earlier and how Blake was acting.

"Oh hey babe, I didn't even notice you woke up. How are you feeling?" asked Blake.

"I'm fine, what did the doctors say?"

"They said that your iron was low and your stress level was extreme which caused you to faint."

"When can I leave?"

"They said hopefully tomorrow. Once your iron levels are better, you can go home." I turned over on my side to get my purse when Blake touched me on the shoulder. I stood still because I

153

didn't know what he was going to do. Blake was iffy today, and I had to be prepared for whatever he was going to throw at me. Even though his actions only were different today, I hated not knowing if he was going to be angry or happy. He was bipolar as hell. It showed, and I didn't know how to respond.

"Baby, what's the matter? I'm not going to hurt you." I turned over and moved his hand off of my shoulder. He looked at me confused and backed up from the bed a little and looked me in the eyes. He had this expression that I had seen a hundred times before.

"Well, the way you've been acting, I am surprised to see you here, or even showing that you care because earlier today you acted as if you hated me and wanted to keep me on lock down."

"Janelle I just don't like you seeing that man, he is interested in you, and I don't want him to try anything crazy with you."

"Blake, do you hear yourself? You cannot keep people from being interested, but as your wife, you should know that I wouldn't even allow that. And plus we spent days together in the hospital months ago. Don't you think he would have tried something there?"

"You're right; maybe I was being overdramatic.''

"And Blake, another thing, you are not going to stop me from seeing my friends when I don't stop you from seeing yours."

"Okay Janelle, I'm sorry." Blake sat back down on the chair next to the window and put on his dark blue Champions hoodie I had gotten him for Christmas a few years ago. I looked over at him and watched him change the channel. After that conversation, we didn't speak the rest of the night.

I hardly slept the whole night because the doctors and nurses kept coming in the room checking on me. One of the nurses came in my room four times just to check my vitals. She drew my blood once around 3:30 a.m. and that was it. I guess it was still low because they were checking my vitals left and right. I was sitting up in the bed watching reruns of Friends when I got a text from Autumn checking to see how I was doing.

Chapter 15

I woke up the next morning around eight, and Blake wasn't in the chair next to the window. I was getting up from the bed to use the bathroom when I noticed a note sitting on the light brown wooden nightstand where the old white hospital phone was sitting. I picked up the note. It was from Blake, "I'm going to grab you some breakfast from the café. I love you." I put the note back down and headed to the bathroom. As I made my way there, I could feel the cold tile floor through my blue hospital socks. I could feel the cold air run through the gown. I hated how they didn't cover up your backside. I could only imagine what kind of underwear the doctors see when the girls walk up and down the halls. I hoped the doctor wasn't going to enter the room because I had on a black thong, and I hated the beauty mark that was on my butt. It was dead smack in the middle of my left cheek. Every time Blake and I had sex; he would always poke at it. That drove me crazy. I went into the bathroom and

156

looked at myself in the mirror and noticed that my hair was dry and matted to my head. My afro was flat on one side of my head, and some of my curls were straight. I quickly put some water on it and then walked over to use the bathroom. Walking back to my bed, I noticed that Blake hadn't returned. I got to the bed, stretched out, and turned on the TV. In the middle of watching television, the doctor came in carrying a bunch of papers and a chart. He looked at the TV for a few seconds and then turned his attention back to me.

"Good morning, Janelle."

"Good morning."

"So the last test we did on you didn't show any signs except that you are very stressed and your iron is low. Other than that, you're fine. Since those few things are normal for you, you are able to go home now."

"Okay, thank you."

"Have a great day, stay stress-free."

"I'll try."

157

Before I was able to get dressed, I had to wait for one of the nurses to come into the room to take out the IVs. I didn't know why it was taking Blake so long to get back with breakfast if he only went downstairs to the café. I got up off of the bed, pushed the alarm for a nurse to come, and went to the other side of the bed to grab my clothes. I was putting on my pants when Blake walked into the room. He knocked on the door and then headed toward me.

"Oh my god, Blake. You scared the crap out of me."

"I'm sorry."

"I thought you went to get us breakfast?"

"I was..."

"So what happened?"

"Umm. Never mind that. Why are you getting dressed?"

"The doctor said I can go home."

"Okay, babe." Blake stood there with this hand in his pockets looking around the room like he had something to do. He kept on looking at his watch.

"Baby, if you have something to do, you can go."

"Janelle, stop being dramatic, just get dressed." I finished getting my clothes on and gathering the things I had laying around the room. Blake was still standing there. He then started pacing the floor, mumbling under his breath. He was talking so fast I couldn't catch what he was saying. The only thing I heard was *killed and I can't*. I didn't know what that meant, but I knew he was stressed about something because of the way he had been acting. In the middle of Blake talking, the nurse came in and looked surprised that I was out of the hospital gown and standing waiting for someone to come in.

"Wow, you're ready to go home, I see."

"Yes, I am." The nurse smiled. She came closer and started removing the IV from my hand and was cleaning up everything.

Before I could get up, Blake was rushing out of the room and didn't even let me know if he was waiting outside in the car or was going to be in the waiting room. Before I could even call his name, he was already out the door.

"Okay sweetie, you are all ready to go."

"Okay, thank you."

I got up off the bed, grabbed my purse, and headed downstairs to find Blake. I was in the hallway down from my room waiting for the elevator to come back up. I looked at my phone and noticed I had gotten a few emails. I clicked on the app and refreshed the page. I had gotten an email from a few clothing stores and another one from Darryl and Doctor Landry. I opened the one from Doctor Landry first because I thought it was strange that he would be sending me an email when he knew my husband's number. He could have just called Blake. The elevator opened, and five people came out holding it's a girl balloons, gifts, stuffed animals and flowers. After it was emptied, I stepped inside and pushed the button to the first floor. I looked back at my phone to read the message that

160

Doctor Landry had sent me; it only said to call him, which was strange. I reached the first floor and headed out of the hospital doors to see if I could see Blake's car. I didn't see it in the front waiting for me. I dialed his number, and as I was calling him, I was also getting a text from Darryl. I didn't look at it because I was waiting for Blake to answer his phone. I waited until the call went to voicemail. I hung up and then called back again. That time he answered on the third ring.

"Where are you?"

"In the parking lot."

"Pull up to the front. How the hell am I supposed to find you in the parking lot?"

"Hold on; I am coming." Blake and his attitude was really getting on my nerves; I didn't know what was going on with him. I was not going to be able to hold my tongue if that continued. I was going to hurt someone's feelings. Blake pulled up to the curb blasting Usher's song, *I Don't Mind.* I opened the car door. As soon as I got in, Blake pulled off out of the parking lot. I ended up dropping my phone and leaning over to the other side.

"Will you slow down?" Blake didn't say anything; he just kept driving. I put on my seat belt and picked up my phone. I opened the text message that Darryl had sent. He was just checking on me and was demanding that I call Dr. Landry and read the email that he had sent me. I looked over at Blake, and he was so focused on the road. I opened the email from Darryl. It read, "Dr. Landry needs to see you ASAP, it's important. Whenever you get a chance, meet him at the address 1437 Crescent Lane. Email him when you can meet him." I didn't know if I should have been worried or not, but I knew it must have been important if he wanted to meet me that bad. I laid back against the seat and looked out of the window. I noticed that we had driven passed the exit to get home. I knew we weren't going to get Junior because we had passed that exit as well. I didn't say anything about it to Blake because I didn't know if he was in one of those moods. I just kept quiet. I started thinking about where everything had gone wrong. What had I done for Blake to be acting so strange? I know I was acting strange the first time we had sex after being away from him for so long, but after that, I was fine. Blake was acting like he was hiding something, and it was all about to fall apart. It had only been a few days, but even that wasn't normal for Blake. He wasn't the stressful type. He always kept himself away from stress and would take the time he needed if something was really bothering him. This time around he was falling, and he didn't want me to catch him. I needed to be the wife, and he wasn't even allowing me to be.

"Blake where are we going?"

"On a vacation."

"Where are we going? Don't we need to pack and get Junior?"

"No we can just buy a few things when we get there, and Junior is staying with my sister for the weekend. I just want us to spend some time alone and get closer. I feel like we are falling apart and it needs to be fixed before it gets worse."

"Okay baby. I love you."

"I love you too, Janelle?"

I turned around, lay back against the seat, and looked out of the window of the car. Blake was changing the radio stations, trying to find one where they weren't talking. When he finally got tired of searching, he turned the radio off and turned on Drake. He loved Drake; he always listened to him. He started picking up speed on 495; there wasn't any traffic, and we cruised most of the way. As the songs changed, I received a call from Doctor Landry. I quickly answered. Before I said hello, I turned down the car stereo. Blake gave me a look, and I motioned that I was on the phone.

"Hello?"

"Oh hey Janelle, how are you?"

"I am fine Doctor Landry. What's up?"

"Did Darryl email you?"

"Yes, he did. I was going to call you later. But what's up?"

"Are you alone?"

"No, I'm with my husband."

"Oh okay, I'll call you back, or you can call me back once you are free."

"Are you sure Doctor Landry?"

"Yes, I am positive."

"Okay, goodbye."

"Bye."

I hung up the phone, and when I looked at Blake, he was already looking at me.

"What?"

"What did Doctor Landry want?"

"I don't know; he said to call him back once I have some free time."

"Okay, babe."

"So Blake where are we going anyway?"

"Why can't you just be surprised?" He smiled.

"Just give me a hint. Is it a hot or cold place? I'm guessing it's a hot place because we are driving there, and it's no more than 16 hours away."

"Well, you just answered all of your hints. Now sit back and relax." I reached over and slapped him on the arm.

"Come on baby, not right now. Save all of that for when we get to our destination. I smiled and lay back down on the seat. I didn't know where we were going, but I knew it was going to be an interesting weekend because Blake was being himself again. However, I didn't know how his attitude would be by the time we got to wherever we were going.

It was 8:00 p.m. and we were near Virginia. I hated driving through Virginia because it was one of the longest states. Blake and I were getting along during the car ride. We laughed, talked about old times, shared a bunch of old memories that only one of us had remembered. I had forgotten how much time we had shared together. It was really nice reminiscing with him. The drive was bringing us closer. We were getting along, and it felt good that we weren't mad at each other or ignoring each other anymore. I loved Blake and didn't want anything to change that at all. I wanted us to have a great and happy marriage after I returned home. I knew there wasn't such a thing as a perfect marriage; so the struggles that we were going through were only going to make us stronger. I didn't want it to pull us apart. I just needed him to talk to me, and I could help him with his stress. Blake really wasn't himself when he was stressed. Once we arrived at our destination, I just wanted us to have a good relaxing weekend. I had fallen asleep around nine and woke up. We were still in Virginia but closer to Virginia Beach. I sat up and looked at Blake; he looked so exhausted. I thought he would fall asleep at any moment.

"Blake, do you want me to drive?"

"No babe, I got this.''

"Blake, let me drive the rest of the way."

"Alright let me pull over." Once he pulled over, we got out and switched seats. I got into the driver's seat, pulled the seat closer to the steering wheel, put on my seat belt, repositioned the mirror, and got back on the highway. Blake put the passenger seat all the way back and stretched out.

"Baby wait." Blake looked up at me.

"Where am I going? I don't want to just keep driving, and we pass the exit."

"Get off at the exit for Virginia Beach."

"We're going there. You could have just said that."

"I wanted it to be a surprise."

"Okay baby, which hotel."

"The Hampton Inn, it's right …"

"I know babe; I remember where it is from the last time we came here." Blake smiled at me then turned on his side facing the door and fell asleep.

I couldn't believe that we were going back to the same place where we had one of the most amazing vacations. We had gone there around the beginning of our relationship. My grandmother did not want me to go unless Jean was going as well She said that Blake was just all talk and could never back anything up. The day I told her that I was going with him for our summer vacation, she almost had a heart attack. Jean ended up coming with us. He didn't follow us around; he just made sure to check on me each day. Blake and I enjoyed ourselves that week. We drew closer, and that's when we both realized that our relationship was going to last. It was funny how different I pictured it. I couldn't believe that we were there again. I was so excited to see how things had changed and how our relationship would change even more.

Chapter 16

I pulled up to the hotel and Blake was snoring with his mouth wide open. I drove closer to the building and found a parking spot near the entrance. I put the car in park and went to wake Blake up when he started stretching.

"Babe, we are here."

Blake lifted himself up, looked out of the window, turned towards me and leaned in to kiss me. I leaned over and kissed him. I turned the car off and got out. Blake got out, walked over to me, grabbed my hand, pulled me closer to his body and smiled. He was thrilled, and that made me excited to see what he had in store for us. We walked into the hotel lobby, walked over to the front desk, and Blake checked us in. The lady at the front desk was wearing a black blazer and a white sheer collared shirt. She had on bright blue eye shadow and red lipstick. She looked like a clown, and I couldn't stop staring, thinking how wrong her makeup was. She had the biggest smile on her face when she handed us the room keys, and Blake told her to have a good night. I thought that she was overly friendly. I wondered if she knew Blake and was mocking me or something. I quickly erased that thought from my mind when Blake pulled me from the desk as he was heading to the elevator. I hated getting into elevators. What made it worse was that the room was on the tenth floor. I couldn't understand why Blake didn't ask for a room that was closer to the bottom. I would have been fine with anything else.

We reached the tenth floor, and the elevator made a low sound. The doors opened, and we walked right up to the suite that was just down the hall. Blake used the key to open the door, and before we went inside, he covered my eyes with his hand. We walked a little further and then Blake took his hands off of me. I opened my eyes and sat on the bed. Blake walked into the bathroom and turned on the shower. I was confused as to why he had me close my eyes because there was nothing romantic.

"Wow, Blake this is really romantic. Sheets." He walked out of the bathroom grinning.

"Now you knew there wasn't going to be any rose petals here. I just wanted to play with your head."

"Well, thanks babe."

"You're welcome." I lay down on the bed and turned on the TV to see what I could watch. I took off my clothes and got comfortable on the bed waiting for Blake to come out.

"Baby, do you want to join me?"

"Blake I hate taking showers with you. No."

"Come on babe; it will be fun, I promise."

"You said that the last time, and I ended up hitting my head on the tiles in our bathroom." Blake started cracking up laughing.

"Oh, shut up. I don't believe that hitting my head and almost passing out is anything to be laughing about." He didn't answer back, so I figured he was in the shower. I got up and put my clothes back on, grabbed my wallet, and headed towards the bathroom to tell Blake that I was running to the gas station to get us something to snack on. I walked out into the warm, humid air and quickly walked across the street. When I went into the gas station, I picked up a few bags of chips, some cupcakes, and a few drinks. I walked over to the counter. The guy behind the register was looking down at his phone and didn't even realize that I was standing there.

"Excuse me, sir."

He looked up at me, looked at his phone, and then started ringing me up. I was wondering what was so interesting on his phone. He kept looking at it while I stood at the counter. He was really into whatever was on the screen. I didn't say anything about him having poor customer service, which I should have because it was horrible. Once he finished ringing me up, I headed back to the hotel. The lady at the front desk was staring at me as I walked over to the elevator. She still had that annoying smile on her face; she didn't say anything to me but kept staring. I wanted to walk over to the front desk and ask her what was up, but I didn't want to get her fired or get kicked out since Blake had planned that getaway for us. I got on the elevator and witnessed a couple arguing about who the guy was texting and calling. The girl was so angry; she pushed his phone out of his hand. The guy picked it up to see if his screen had cracked. The girl that he was with kept on screaming that he was nothing but a worthless nigga, and he just stared at the wall in the elevator like he didn't even hear a word she was saying. She then smacked him in the face, and he was about to hit her back when he saw that I was watching him. He put his hand down and pushed her to the other side. She ended up flying past me when the elevator door opened. When the couple finally made it out of the elevator, I quickly walked down the hall to my room. I reached our room and realized that I had left the room key. Banging on the door for a few minutes until Blake finally answered, he opened the door half way. When I walked in, I noticed that he was walking over to the bed naked.

"Babe, really?"

"What?" He turned around and smiled.

174

The Truth in Every Lie

I couldn't help but smile back. I walked over to the bed, dropped the bag, and started taking off my clothes. Blake leaned in and kissed me on the neck. He laid me down on the bed and caressed my breast. Blake had this weird thing about breast where he had to touch them before we had sex. As Blake kept on kissing me, I started thinking about the night we first had sex. It was right there, at the same hotel. It might have even been the same room.

Chapter 17

By the time we arrived home from our mini-vacation, I had already made an appointment to see Doctor Landry the next day because I wanted to see what exactly he needed to talk to me about. Blake was getting some of the bags out of the car when our front door opened. An officer was coming out holding up a badge and a piece of paper. I got out of the car, and Blake let go of the bags and walked over to the cop.

"Excuse me officer, may we help you?"

"Yes, I am Officer Michael Reid and Sir you are under …" Blake jumped into the car and sped down the street. The officer tried to chase after him. He turned back around and tried to pull off.

"Wait!" He put the car in park and pulled the car back into the driveway.

"He's gone; you aren't going to catch him." He got out of the car and walked over toward me.

"Do you know where he might be going?"

"How would I know, all of this is new to me. I am in complete shock at what you are telling me.

"If you hear from him, can you call me?"

"No." The officer looked at me like I had said something out of the ordinary.

No, what do you mean ma'am? The officer asked puzzled.

"Can you tell me why you are looking for my husband and why his ass just sped out of the driveway?"

"We were given information that your husband murdered someone about a year ago, and we have been looking for him."

"What? My husband didn't kill anyone. You must have the wrong guy."

"Miss, if I had the wrong guy, then why did your husband drive off?"

"Maybe he's in trouble for something else, but murder just doesn't sound like Blake."

"Whether your husband did or didn't actually murder someone, he still has a warrant out for his arrest and we will find him."

"Officer Reid, can you please contact me if you guys find him and arrest him?

"Yes, we sure can. I will contact you as soon as possible."

I walked away from the police officer and headed into the house. I couldn't believe that Blake was wanted for murder. I mean, whether or not he did it or not, he was still wanted. Maybe that's what Doctor Landry wanted to tell me. I needed it to be morning already so that I could talk to him. The whole thing was stressing me out. I went into our bedroom to plug in my phone. When it finally turned on, I had five miss calls from Blake. I jumped off of the bed and quickly called him back. He was breathing heavy, and by the sound of it, he was still in the car because he had the music blasting.

"Blake, turn the music down. I can't hear anything that you are saying."

"Baby, I am so sorry."

"Sorry for what? Did you really kill someone?"

"Babe, I can't talk about it right now, they might have the phones crossed."

"Well, when in hell do you expect to be telling me about this? At my funeral!"

"Janelle, this is not funny; I am wanted for murder."

"No. You know what's not funny? That my husband ran from the police and he won't tell me anything about this so called murder."

"I love you; I have to go."

Before I could say anything else, he hung up the phone. I had never felt so sick in my life except for the time when I found out my brother had been murdered and how strange Blake had acted. I thought about how he didn't move a muscle or didn't want to come with me to my grandmother's. He used some lame excuse about my grandparents not liking him. I thought that was a bunch of bull, but I let it go. I did remember how the officer working on my case informed me that the driver was in a black car, but it couldn't have been him because he said part of the evidence was an acrylic nail or whatever. I thought about calling that detective and asking him if he had any more information on Jean's case, but it was Sunday. I remembered that he was off on Sundays. I got out my laptop and started looking for clues in Blake's email. Blake had two Gmail accounts. I knew the passwords just in case he ever forgot them or if something happened, I would be able to get information for him. I wanted to see if he had evidence of any murder. When I logged into the account, it said that he was logged on somewhere else, so I got up from the bedroom and walked over to his office. I went to the door and stared at it for a moment. Then I went to turn the knob, but

it was locked. I went downstairs, grabbed a butter knife, and ran

back up the steps to unlock the door. Wedging the knife in between

the door and the lock, I finally popped it open. I dropped the knife

on the floor. As I was walking over to his desk, I noticed he had a

bunch of papers laying on the sofa by the window. I walked over to

it and started looking through the papers. The only things in that pile

were law firm cases and a book. I fumbled through some of his

notebooks and workbooks to see if there were any loose papers. I

hated having to go through his things, but I really wanted to know if

I could find anything that lead up to him murdering anyone. I

thought hard about what my life would be like if he had murdered

someone. I thought about losing Junior, or better yet, having to

spend time in jail for something stupid. I couldn't take another trip

back to the mental institution or jail. I knew for a fact that I was not

strong enough to do prison time. I walked over to his desk and

turned on his laptop. I couldn't get into it because he had a password

set. That was strange. All of the years we'd been married, I had all of his passwords, and he never had a password on his computer.

That had to have been recent, when I was away. I tried putting my

name, Junior's name, his parent's name, and even his sister's. After

the first few tries, the computer locked itself. Since I couldn't get

into his computer, I went into the closet where he kept a few suits

and more books. When I opened it, I was hit in the head with a bat.

It had rolled off of the shelf with some rope tied around it. I had

pulled up a chair to get to the top shelf when I saw a black suitcase

with a white tag that read *No Longer Exist*. I pulled down the

suitcase and sat it on the floor. I also pulled out a notebook and a

shoe box from underneath it. I sat down on the chair and opened the

notebook. The first couple of pages were empty, and flipping

through the book; I came across a few writings that said his name.

There was one particular page that had all of the lines filled in; there

were actually a few pages like that. I pulled the pages out of the

book and through the book on the floor. The first page said

something about how much he wanted to get revenge on someone,

about how he hated him for what he had done, and about how his revenge was soon to happen. I started crying. I knew that I was jumping to conclusions, but I didn't know what else to think. I didn't know of any serious beef that my brother and Blake had since they were actually good friends. I changed thoughts for a second because I needed to find some evidence, and I didn't even know if he had truly killed my brother. I folded those papers up and placed them on my lap. I then opened a Nike shoe box, and it was filled with old papers from college, cards, and things from our wedding. I dumped everything out of the box and looked past a few papers. There was a key. It was a small and silver, and it had the number 656 on it. I didn't know what that meant or what the key was for; I got tired of looking through Blake's things and went into the bedroom. I walked over to my phone; I didn't have any missed calls or text messages. I went into the bathroom and ran some water to take a bath. I couldn't find the soap that I loved using whenever I was stressed, so I used one of those perfume smelling bath balls that I got for Christmas from a co-worker. Sitting on the edge of the toilet seat, I heard my phone ringing and quickly got up and ran into the bedroom. When I looked at my phone, I saw that it was Darryl. I picked up, and he automatically started talking.

"Hey Janelle, how are you? Are you busy?"

"No Darryl, what's up?"

"Just checking up on you. I haven't heard from you since we met at Panera."

"I'm fine; I just have a few things on my mind."

"Anything you want to talk about?"

"No, not really."

I hung up the phone before Darryl could even say another word. After throwing my phone on the bed, I heard my doorbell rang. I didn't know who was at my front door because I wasn't expecting anyone. I quickly went back into the bathroom and turned off the running water. I ran down the steps. Once I got to the end of the steps, the ringing stopped. I could see that the person was wearing a red top and black bottoms. I opened the front door to find a woman standing there with a motorcycle helmet and a black leather jacket. The helmet was all black and had a bunch of stickers on it. I also noticed there was a name on it. Before I could read the rest of the name, the young woman cleared her throat and shifted her body to the left.

"Oh I'm sorry, can I help you?"

"Yes, is Blake here?"

"He's in the shower, can I help you?"

"I am an old friend from college; I was in town to see family, so I decided to stop on by."

"Oh I'm sorry, he must've forgotten. I will tell him you stopped by and make sure he calls you. What is your name?"

"Do you mind if I just wait until he comes out?"

"Well, I do mind. I don't know who you are, and I am busy right now. It would be highly appreciated if you just come back.'' I went to close the door when she blocked it with her foot. I opened the door back up, and she was holding out a gun. She had the gun aiming at me. She walked into the house and walked behind me, still pointing the gun toward me.

"Excuse me? Who did you say you were again?"

"None of your business, where is the bathroom?"

"Blake isn't here. If you were really his friend, you guys would have talked before you came over."

"Listen Janelle, do not get smart with me. Where is your husband?"

"No disrespect lady, but if you want me to even acknowledge you, I need you to put the damn gun down."

"Girl, would you just tell me where the hell Blake is. This is not a game. Do you think this is a joke?"

"No, but I am damn sure not going to allow someone to come into my home and tell me what I should be doing. One thing you need to know is that I don't back down from anything."

186

"Shut the hell up!" I moved away from my front door and started walking over to the kitchen.

"Where the hell do you think you are going?"

"In my damn kitchen to call the police or you can already leave and go looking for my husband because he's not here." This woman had some nerve coming into my house trying to boss me around. I don't know why she thought I was supposed to be afraid of her; she was not a threat to anyone.

"Janelle I will be back in a couple of days and if you see your husband tell him I am looking for him and I want my damn money." The woman was walking towards the front door when she knocked over one of the end table lamps. She giggled a little bit, then opened the door and walked out. She left the front door open. When I went to close the door, she was getting on her motorcycle. She fixed her ponytail and then threw on her helmet. Once she pulled out of the driveway, I closed the door and headed to the kitchen. I got out the broom and dustpan, cleaned up the broken navy blue lamp that my grandmother gave me.

Chapter 18

I woke up around noon and was in the same spot from the night before. I sat up thinking about how I'd be spending more nights without my husband. I hated the fact that he was wanted for murder and I didn't even see it coming. I thought I knew him like the back of my hand, but I was wrong. It hurt so bad knowing that my man was even capable of murdering someone. Blake had a temper that could get out of hand but to kill someone; I didn't know he even had it in him. I thought I was the crazy one, but it looked like I was wrong. I didn't have it in my heart to call or text Blake.

I went upstairs into our bedroom and picked out something to wear. I walked into our closet and chose a black lace top that was behind my favorite romper, I was going to put that on, but I decided just to grab a pair of boyfriend jeans. I went into the bathroom and let out the water from the previous night. I turned on the water and got into the shower. It was extremely hot and felt so good running on my skin. I was so tense that it started to loosen me up a little. I stood under the shower nozzle until the water started to get cool. I couldn't help but think about everything that was happening in my life. It was falling apart every day. I was figuring out the truth about my husband, my family, old friends, my sex life, being jobless, and even not being able to speak to my grandparents. I didn't want to stop keeping in contact with them, but after having my son and being admitted into a mental institution, I couldn't help it. I was embarrassed. In addition, Blake being wanted for murder made me lose my faith. I didn't know what else could happen.

I got out of the shower, and it was almost 1:00 p.m. I threw my clothes on and tied my hair into a bun and headed out the door. When I was closing the door, I noticed a guy outside of the house just standing there. He was holding a brown box. I walked over to my car and got inside; I looked out of the rearview mirror, and the guy was walking over to me. I quickly locked the doors and turned the ignition. He came up to the window and motioned his hands for me to roll it down. I rolled down the window just enough to hear what he was saying.

"Hi Janelle, my name is Johnathan. Blake sent me over to give you this package. He said he would have called or even came by but he is still hiding and didn't want to chance anything just yet." I rolled down my window even more and grabbed the box. While I it, the guy kept standing there. I looked at him, and he didn't move or even stop watching. I was getting a little nervous. When I opened the box, there was a smaller box inside, I took it out and threw the other box into the back seat. I lifted the top off. There was a gold bracelet with a gold charm. I took a closer look at the charm. It was a heart with an imprinted capital J on it. I put the bracelet back into the box, put my car in drive, and pulled out of my driveway. Racing down the street, not noticing the stop sign, I ran right through and almost got hit by another car. Looking in my rearview, I saw that the car was stopped at the intersection. I kept driving to the highway, blasting K. Michelle. On the way to meet with Doctor Landry, I couldn't help but think about what he was going to tell me. I knew he would probably tell me about how he had found out that Blake

had killed my brother, but little did he know, I already knew.

Driving up to Doctor Landry's office, I noticed that I had

three missed calls and two text messages from Blake and one missed

call and a text from Darryl. I didn't respond to either of them and

just headed up to the office. It resembled the hospital where he

worked. The walls were white with blue trimmings. He had little to

no paintings hanging them, and there were several rooms. Each door

had a sign that said employees only until I reached the door at the

end of the hall. I walked into the office and was automatically

greeted by his secretary. She had dirty blonde hair and wore a red

shirt with blue jeans. She had the biggest smile cn her face. She

came from behind her desk to shake my hand. The woman was way

too friendly to be a secretary. I shook her hand. Then she told me to

take a seat and that Doctor Landry would be with me once he

finished with his patient. I sat close to the door so that it was easier

to see him come out of his office.

I was there to find out the truth of all lies. I knew I had a big pill to swallow; I was ready to take it. I carried extra water with me and could take whatever. I was twenty-five years old and facing things you only see in movies or seasons of Law & Order. It bothered me knowing that I was falling and Blake wasn't here to catch me. I was falling off a cliff. I kept falling and still hadn't hit the ground. All I could do was watch my life fall apart until I awoke from that horrible dream. Doctor Landry came out of his office wearing his white button up shirt and a pair of light blue jeans. He looked across the room and waved at me. I got up from the chair and walked towards his office. My heart was pounding, and my hands started to sweat. Wiping my hands on my jeans, I could feel the uncomfortable vibe in the room. He opened up the windows that had a perfect view of the city. I watched him look out of the window for a few minutes while I tried shaking the nervousness and stopping my hands from sweating so much. Breaking the silence, he mumbled something under his breath.

"Excuse me, Doctor Landry?"

"Janelle, this is really hard for me to tell you this. Before I knew you, I was only in it for the money, but once I got to know you, treating you was a lot harder for me. I never meant to hurt you."

"What do you mean? I don't understand what you're telling me."

Doctor Landry walked over toward the sofa where I was sitting. He looked at the wall behind me.

"Doctor Landry say something."

"Janelle, I am so sorry; I'm so sorry."

"I swear if you don't start explaining yourself."

"Blake paid me to admit you into my mental institution; you don't have multiple personality disorder. The night you supposedly went crazy, Blake had given you a pill that made you feel and act different. It was created by a good friend of mine for people with a disorder. The pill usually relaxes them, but in your case, it did the opposite. I had him give it to you during your pregnancy so that it would work and the side effects would kick in correctly." As Doctor

Landry was explaining everything to me, I couldn't figure out why Blake would want me to think I had a disorder.

"Hold on a minute, so you're saying there is nothing wrong with me?"

"Well yes, I only had you stay for the time you did because we needed you to create something in your head and add it to your chart, but after that we stopped the medication. Blake wanted to blame you for something he had done but he knew he needed you to be out of your mind. After the first few weeks, I was making a lot of money working for him because you told him that Sasha (your other personality) had confessed to murdering your parents and that put the icing on the cake."

"Everything you are telling me is a joke, right? This all sounds like a movie, and I'm the dummy believing you."

"I'm sorry Janelle; I'm sorry, but this is all true. Please let me finish." I put my feet up on the sofa and looked Doctor Landry in the face while he continued to tell me everything.

"Do you remember the day I told you that you could go home?"

"Yes I do, it was the best day of my life."

"Well, Blake called me the night before and told me that he had handled his problem and wanted me to tell you that you could go home. He still wanted you to take the medicine so that you would believe that you really had an issue and wouldn't figure out what was happening. I didn't want to send you home without you knowing the truth.

"No, you didn't want to stop getting your money; you didn't care about me."

"Janelle, yes I did, that's why I had Darryl become your shrink. He knew that there was nothing wrong with you but didn't know the deal Blake and I had.

"Please shut up; I need to think. So your telling me that all of you guys were in on this and it didn't cross none of your minds that I would be affected. I really trusted you Dr. Landry and all you did was prove to me that you are just like my husband. I can't even sit here and look at you. I can't believe anything you say."

I lay back on the leather sofa and stared up at the ceiling trying to put everything he had told me in order. My husband was blaming me for something instead of him owning up to it and dealing with the consequences. At that very moment, I hated Blake. Everything that had happened between us was irrelevant. Blake was dead to me. Deep down I knew I loved him, but at that moment, I couldn't think of him without wanting to throw up.

"Janelle, are you okay?''

"Did he kill my brother?"

"What?"

"Did Blake kill my brother? Is that what he wanted to blame on me?"

"Janelle, I have no idea about that. We never talked about what it was that he wanted to blame on you. We only discussed you and what we had in store for you."

196

"Is there anything else you need to tell me? Because I need to know before I walk out of this office and never talk to you again."

"Yes, there is more." I looked over at Doctor Landry; he was picking at his nails and fumbling with the creases in his jeans. When he finally looked up at me, he burst into tears. He was weeping. I sat up and looked at him.

"Doctor Landry, come on you can tell me."

"I was the one who told the police about Blake. I told them a few things but not everything." I jumped up off of the sofa.

"Are you telling me that you told the police about Blake but not your side? You're a sorry excuse of a doctor, not a man. That's insane." I was about to say something else when three police officers came running in.

"Mr. Landry you are under arrest for helping a murderer; you have the right to remain silent. If you do say anything, what you say can be used against you in a court of law."

"Hello miss, I am sorry you had to witness this but if you don't mind can you please exit the building."

"Can you tell me what's going on, I know why you are arresting him but how did you find that information out."

"What do you mean you know why hes being arrested? Were you involved?"

"No, well yes but in the way you are thinking. Blake is my husband, hes the guy who murdered my brother and that's how I know Dr. Landry."

"Do you know where your husband is right now?"

"No I don't, he's been on the run since the last time I saw him. But how did you know Dr. Landry was involved?"

"Between me and you, we got a call from someone working with your husband and Dr. Landry and gave us some good information about what's been going on. So we took the chance to see if we could catch Dr. Landry and we did. I'm sorry all of this is happening but if you see your husband tell him we are looking for him. it would be better for all of us If he just turned himself in. And I'm sorry for your loss."

Once the officers were gone, I picked up my belongings. The friendly secretary was no longer sitting at her desk. They must've arrested her as well.

Chapter 19

Waking up the next morning with Blake lying next to me was pretty scary. He was sleeping so peaceful, lying on our bed like he wasn't wanted for murder and could get arrested any day. I didn't remember him coming home, getting into the bed or even changing clothes. I got up from the bed and went into Junior's room to see if he was still sleeping. He wasn't. I got him up and put him in the tub to get washed up. Every day I worried about losing my son; I worried if Blake really loved me or even if I was going to jail for what he had done. The possibilities were endless because I could one day be murdered by my husband, be homeless, and become a drug addict, or even not be able to ever work again. I hated the fact that I couldn't keep my son safe, and he couldn't help what he was born into. For the first few months, he was without a mother. Then he had to spend a few weeks with his aunt or at a babysitter. I hadn't spent time with him; we hadn't bonded. The one thing I ever wanted for my son was for him to live a good life and have a better childhood

than I had. My childhood wasn't bad, but I wanted him to always

feel loved, to not want for anything, and to love the both of his

parents. I couldn't bare having my son grow up without his father. I

never wanted to end up that baby mother that had to always bring

her kid to visit their father in jail. That was the last thing I wanted

for Junior's life, but life was speeding past all three of us and

everything I said I wouldn't do was happening.

Junior was going to Blake's sister's house, and I didn't want

to drop him off because I didn't want to miss the opportunity to talk

to Blake about what had really happened. I also wanted to know why

he seemed to have confessed to my brother's murder by giving me a

freaking charm with his initials on it. It wasn't a heartwarming

gesture; it was actually creepy as hell, and it had been in the car

since I received it that day in the driveway. After taking Junior out

of the tub, I brought him into the bedroom and lay him on the bed.

He was smacking his father in the head, and Blake finally woke up.

He stared at me, and all I could do was walk away. Blake called out my name, and I kept walking. Blake must have been out of his mind

thinking I wanted to talk to him while our son was in the room. I

really wanted to know what he had to say, but not like that, not with

our son or even in our bed.

I called Blake's sister to come and pick up Junior so that

Blake couldn't get a chance to leave, and I wanted her to see him

before he was eventually arrested. I figured she would be angry with

me if I didn't let her see him before that. She didn't know our

situation, and she didn't need to know what was going on when I

was still trying to figure it out myself. I needed to know why he did

what he did. Blake wasn't going to get off easy; I was going to make

him feel what I was feeling. A couple of minutes after I was in the

kitchen making a bottle for Junior, Blake came down the stairs

holding him. Junior was holding onto his dad's neck laughing. He

looked so happy with him; He truly loved him. However, what I

knew about my husband made me feel sick to my stomach. Blake

had caused those things to happen to our family. I thought that he

loved us, but all of the secrets were making me not want to keep loving him. He had taken our vows to the next level, and I didn't know if I could stick to them.

Blake walked into the kitchen and gave Junior his bottle. He swiftly took the bottle and started drinking it. I watched Blake bring him into the living room. He sat him on the couch with some of his toys. Blake came up behind me and grabbed my waist, and I quickly moved to the other side of the kitchen, picking up the dishes. He came back towards me and pulled my arm to turn around to look at him. I didn't want to be touched by him or even to look at him even though he was standing next to me, in the same house, and the same room. I didn't want him in my life. Before, I felt lost, but at that moment, I was feeling nothing but hatred.

"Janelle? Stop the bull shit and talk to me."

"What Blake? What?"

"Janelle, I know you're upset and confused, but please let me explain. I love you."

"You love me. Okay. And what do you need to explain, I know you killed my brother, tried to make me seem crazy, and tried to put the blame on me and not yourself. So please save the I love you bull shit. You're a liar."

"Let me explain what happened. I'm so sorry."

"Blake shut up! I don't want to talk right now. Our son is in the other room, and I don't want him hearing us. I'm angry and might say something I shouldn't. Leave me alone."

Blake walked out of the kitchen, and I heard him slam our bedroom door. I went into the living room and waited for his sister to come. I lay on the couch with Junior not knowing if that would be my last time holding him. Junior was my love. Even though he and I hadn't bonded, I knew he loved me too.

Blake came down the steps in only his boxers and Junior's packed bags. He came into the living room, put the bags down, opened the front door, and waited for the person outside to come into the house.

"Is your sister here?" Blake shook his head and looked away. I got up from the couch and grabbed a few of my son's toys for him to play with.

"Hey Janelle, how are you?"

"I'm good girl, how are you?"

"I'm good. So is everything packed?"

"Yes, Blake's putting everything in the car. Girl thank you for being able to take him for a few days; I really do appreciate it."

"No problem, you know I love spending time with my nephew."

Blake came back into the house and grabbed the car seat. I picked up Junior and carried him to the car. Blake and his sister were talking while he was putting the car seat inside. I stood behind him until he finished strapping in the seat.

"I got it babe, give me him." I smiled at Blake, kissed Junior goodbye, and handed him to his father.

"Sis, Nelly swears she can do it all. I try to tell her that she needs to rest and let me help her. She doesn't even let me change him."

"You two are so cute; I love you guys."

"If she really knew how we were living, she wouldn't love us anymore," I thought to myself. After Blake had strapped Junior inside, his sister got into the car. I was waving goodbye to Junior. I backed away from the car, and Blake leaned forward and put his arm around me.

"Baby brother keep taking care of her, treat her right."

"Sis, you know I am and always will."

I laughed a little under my breath and then Blake kissed me. I didn't want to not kiss him back and have his sister worried or in our business, so I returned a kiss. We waited in the driveway until she backed out and beeped the horn as she drove down the street. Standing there with Blake's hands on me made me sick, so I moved from under his arm and started walking into the house. He grabbed

206

me by the arm and pulled me close to him. He grabbed my chin and kissed me again. I kept kissing him as well. I know how stupid that sounds, but I felt some of the hatred fade. I pulled away and walked into the house. I went into the bedroom and lay down on the bed. I grabbed the remote off of the nightstand and turned on some daytime television. Blake came up a few minutes later with a bowl of cereal. I watched him get in the bed munching on the cereal. He was acting like nothing had happened. He just sat there and watched me flip through the channels.

Chapter 20

Blake's confession

"Blake I am sick and tired of asking you the same damn questions. Why is it so hard for you to just tell me what happened and why you did it? I am not asking to confess on a stand and throw you in jail. I'm asking because I am your wife and you betrayed me. that's the least you could do."

As I watched Blake go through the closet and pick out clothes for him to wear I couldn't help but want to throw the remote that was on the bed. Blake was making me extremely angry.

"Blake can you answer my question!"

"Janelle I don't know what you want me to say right now."

He turned back around and left the room. I got up and followed him to his office, he was sitting on the couch and was looking through some of the notebooks in a box.

"You know what you can start off by saying?"

"What Nells, what?"

"Don't call me Nells, I need you to answer these questions and anything else you would like to confess up too." Blake looked up from the book and stared at me. It was like he wanted to say something but he didn't. He just kept staring at me.

"I swear if you don't answer my questions." I got silent trying to keep myself from walking up to him and slapping him in his face. I had to try to cool myself down because I didn't want this to get out of hand and then something bad happened.

"Janelle I am so sorry about what I did to you and our family. I didn't intend for us to get here. Well, I mean I didn't want you to find out that I had killed your brother. I wasn't planning on blaming this on you at all until the girl I was going to blame found out that I

was planning to get rid of her; she threatened to turn me in to the

police, so I paid her off and made her leave the state. Once I didn't

have anyone else to point this and the detective had that clue of the

fake nail, I had to blame it on another woman. I know you are

probably thinking why I chose you. Well, because you're my wife,

you were easy to fool. I put a lot of thought into first. I met Doctor

Landry way back in college and he owed me a favor. Once he heard

that I would pay him, he was all in. He knows a few people who can

switch meds and create them into a drug that doesn't harm your

body but makes you bug out. I started putting it into your breakfast

or drinks depending on the night or your mood. I started you on the

pill during your pregnancy. The pill makes you think you are

someone else without you waking up realizing what happened

before. I never thought about what would happen if you found out

that you weren't really sick or how I killed your brother. It crossed

my mind every single day. I even wanted to tell you the plan and

maybe you would have seen the good in me and would understand. I know you're probably ready to hear why I killed your brother. To be honest babe, I am a little nervous about telling you what happened between your brother and I. It was over something that seemed big at the time, but now that my back is against the wall, it seems so minor. I should have never taken this route and should have been the bigger person. The day you found out that your brother had died, I was afraid that you would have picked up that I was the killer, but you didn't. I felt extremely horrible having to sit with this on my heart. I watched you grieve all of that time. I know it hurts you even more knowing who murdered him. I don't want you to forgive me right now, but if you can someday, it would be less painful for the both of us. I know you hate me right now, but I love you and want you to remember all of the good times we shared over the years."

"Blake I need you to tell me why you murdered my brother; I need to know what went wrong with you guys and why you felt that killing him was your only option. I need to know this and why you chose me because I can't believe that you still love me or that you had my best interest at heart."

"Janelle, I do love you."

"Please Blake."

"This might upset you, but while we were together, I cheated on you and got another woman pregnant. It was a one-time thing with her, but I guess my karma caught up with me. I broke it off right after we slept together, but she was sending me emails about how she was pregnant and how she wanted to take me to court and tell you everything. I knew I didn't want you to find out that way and didn't want you to find out from the other woman. I was going to confess, but she told your brother, and he was going to tell you. He wouldn't give me the chance to talk to you first. He kept trying over and over, but I wouldn't let him. Do you remember the time when we were home for the house warming party; we were in the backyard by the grill, and Jean came over making jokes about me having a baby momma somewhere in town? Well, that day I was going to let him tell you everything since he had started a war. Then I looked at you, and your whole mood changed, and I joked it off because I didn't want to hurt you during the party. I thought you deserved to hear it from me. I tried telling you a few times but every time still felt like the wrong time. At that point, Jean was planning to tell you since you didn't go running home to him about what had happened, so I planned to get rid of him for a while so that I could tell you. The night I killed him was not on purpose. I really just meant to hurt him, but something happened, and Jean was just lying there lifeless. I promise you, Janelle. I had no intentions on killing him, and I couldn't go help him because I didn't want to end up in jail or leave you. I didn't want to put you through that. The only reason why I chose you was because I knew if I started taking the pills you wouldn't have anyone to grieve with, that you were going to be all alone. I didn't want me leaving to also be an issue, I didn't want you to raise our son without me in the beginning. I knew you would be a wreck and wouldn't be able to handle raising our son and I was in that mental institution. Yes, I know you have your cousin, but I also know you guys don't talk about everything. I knew we were a couple, and if we were to ever end, one of us would be lost somewhere. We needed each other. Well, I needed you. You might not know this, but I wouldn't be here at this moment without you. I never wanted us to get here, and this was my fault. If I could go back in time, I would change everything, but I can't, so I'm dealing with it. Janelle whatever happens, I want you to know that I will always be here for you and Junior. I transferred most of my money into the joint account and will have Rashaad keep in touch and to help you with whatever you need. I don't know if I will still be running or if they will find me, but before that happens, I want you to be good and not have to struggle because of me. If you need to work, the office has a spot open for you whenever you feel like you need it. I paid the mortgage for the next six months, and I arranged for my things to be put in storage if you were going to move on or just wanted my things gone for a while. Janelle I do plan on turning myself in, but I needed you to know the truth, and I wanted to make sure my family was going to be okay before I left. I love you babe; please look at me."

I waited for Janelle to look at me with warm eyes, but I got cold ones instead. I knew this was not going to be an easy route, but I wanted it to be. Watching my wife sitting there clueless the whole time, made me realize that I had messed up a good thing and if I was ever able to get out of jail, I didn't want her to hate me. I didn't want our relationship to end that way. I put the bowl of cereal on the nightstand behind me and grabbed Janelle and pulled her close. She resisted at first, but I didn't let her go. Then she calmed down and let me hold her. I held her tight against my chest so she could feel my heart beat. For a while, she cried in my arms and didn't say a word. She cried for a few hours while we lay in the bed with everything off.

Chapter 21

After listening to Blake tell me how much he loved me and how he never meant to really hurt me was nice, but I was still mad. Laying down in the bed with him was what I wanted, but he needed to know that I was extremely angry and wanted him out of my life for a while so I could think about our situation a lot more. I needed to be there for my son and wanted to have a clear mind to get myself together. I knew Blake and I would still have a good friendship because of our son, but I knew that I wouldn't forget what he had done. He hurt me, and he needed to know that life could be messy, and messy situations weren't easy to fix. After all, he did kill my brother and wanted the blame to fall on me. I couldn't forgive him so easily because in some ways I hated him. *"Love is pain,* Right?" I hated that saying because whoever said it was an idiot. Why would anyone want love if it was meant to hurt you? It must have been someone who didn't want to leave their child's father after he had cheated multiple times. It was really a saying that a dumb girl in high school would use as an excuse, "But you know *love is pain*, and I am supposed to love my man at all times." I couldn't sit in his arms any longer. Each second that I thought about what he told me made me sick to my stomach. I tried to get up, and he was pulling me back down.

"Blake let me get up; I can't lie here acting like we're still a happy family. You hurt me, and I need my space."

"Janelle, I love you."

"Blake shut up! I know you love me, but I hate you."

I got up off of the bed and went to find something to busy myself with. I grabbed my phone and left the room. I went into the basement and took the bag of laundry downstairs and put them in the washer. I was putting the laundry soap in the dispenser when my phone started ringing. I didn't look at the number and just answered it.

"Hello?"

"Hey Janelle, are you okay?"

"Darryl?"

"Yes, are you okay?"

"Yes I'm okay, I'm trying to stay strong."

"Do you want to talk about it?"

"No, can we talk about something else?"

"Sure, what did you do today?"

"Well, it involves why I'm not in a good mood. My husband is here, and he explained everything to me and what his motives were and blah blah blah."

"Oh okay, well get dressed. I'm going to come over and bring you over to my place. We can watch movies like old times; I miss you. I mean I miss your company."

"I miss you too Darryl."

"So I'll be over around three o clock, is that fine?"

"Yes that's fine, see you soon."

"Bye."

I hung up the phone and went upstairs to see Blake walking into his office. I walked passed the door and went into the bedroom. I picked out a black pair of ripped jeans and a white tank top. I started getting dressed and realized all of my bras were in the

laundry except for an old beat up one that I had for years. It probably

didn't fit anymore. I didn't want to cancel with Darryl, and didn't

have another shirt I could wear without a bra. I jumped into the

shower, and Blake came in staring at me. I didn't know what he was

thinking, but I knew he wanted something because he never said

anything. I was washing my hair. A few minutes later, I felt Blake

standing behind me rubbing my back. I couldn't believe he wanted

sex knowing that I hated him and didn't want to be bothered. I

finished washing the conditioner out, and Blake just stood there

grinning like a freaking little kid. He had the corny smile he used

whenever I was mad at him. For some reason, it always made me

smile. You know how every girl has that one guy she loved that

could get her to rob a bank if he needed her too. Well, Blake was

mine. He and I always had great sex; we often had sex in the

backyard or tried something new. If Blake and I didn't love sex so

much, I could have easily told him to get out and finished taking a shower with no problem, but I couldn't let him leave me and not

have sex with him.

When I finally got out of the shower, someone was ringing

the doorbell, and I had a feeling that it was Darryl. I didn't hear

Blake in the bedroom or getting up to answer the door, so he mustve

left. I didn't know where he could have went that fast. I thought he

would be keeping a low profile since he was wanted but I guess that

didn't matter to him. I quickly got ready and put on my clothes.

When I finally finished getting dressed, I headed downstairs, putting

my wet hair in a top knot bun. Darryl was standing on the outside of

the door. I opened the door to see Darryl's bright white smile.

"Hey Darryl, let me grab my keys. Then I'll be ready to go."

"Okay, I'll be in the car waiting for you."

Darryl and I drove in silence most of the way. He lived in the next

town, over by my cousin's house. When we pulled up the driveway,

I couldn't believe how beautiful his house was. He had a two story

home, a huge driveway, and the lawn was perfect. I got out of the car and waited for him to get something out of his trunk. He walked over to me with a few bags and then headed to the porch.

"Are these both of your houses?"

"Yes, unfortunately, no one lives next door. I've tried getting a tenant, but no one is good to live there."

"You can make yourself comfortable, let me put this in the kitchen." I sat down on the couch, took my sandals off, and rested my feet on his sofa. I could tell he had been single for a long time because his living room décor was a hot mess. He didn't have anything that matched. The couch and the love seat were different, and the lamps he had didn't match the curtains. He really needed help decorating. I was sitting on the sofa waiting for him to return when he came back in with a stack of movies and a few snacks. He came over and handed me the bowl of popcorn and grabbed the remote to turn on the TV.

"So what do you want to watch?"

"Anything, you choose," I said. Darryl got up and opened his shelf and started looking through his selection of movies. He had so many movies; I swear he had to have over a hundred of them just on those few shelves. I bet he had more somewhere else.

"How about we watch Battleship?'' Darryl recommended.

"Okay sure that's fine," I responded. He walked over and put in the movie and sat back on the couch.

"Janelle, why are you still putting up with your husband? Why won't you turn him in?"

"I thought we were going to watch a movie?"

"I'm sorry."

"Don't be, but let's watch the movie. We can talk after."

"Okay."

Sitting there with Darryl wasn't supposed to be about Blake and my current situation. I wanted it to be stress-free. Maybe we could have had sex, get drunk or anything for that matter. I just wanted to forget about Blake and all of the issues he had caused me. Blake had really put me in a tough situation. If Blake's case captured the news eyes, it would blow all of my chances of a normal life. It was going to be hard finding a job, make friends, or even finding someone else to spend the rest of my life with. I didn't want to think

about not being with Blake anymore. He and I had been together for

way too long for me to not even have some type of love for him. No

matter what happens. You have to sometimes forgive and forget.

Life would go on even if I wanted it to go back to where it went

wrong. They both would have still been in my life.

Chapter 22

I didn't really enjoy the movie because I spent the entire time thinking about turning Blake in, or wondering if I should turn myself in just so that Junior would still be able to see his father. Junior would be better off with his father. They had the best chemistry that a father and son could have. Junior was young, but he didn't look at me the way he looked at his father. Being in that hospital wasn't the best thing for me or my son because it caused me to lose everything from my life and within myself. Knowing that everything was a lie was a little hard to get over, and I wasn't okay with knowing the truth, but in due time I hoped it passed and I could move on with my life.

"Janelle, can we talk?"

"Yeah sure, I know you've been waiting for the movie to be over for the longest.''

"You know I have nothing but love for you and you know that I am not trying to hurt you in any way, but sometimes I can't help but wonder why you are even putting up with him."

"Simply because I love him. Stop looking at me like that, you know it's not easy to give up on someone you have been with for such a long time. You try everything in your power to give up on them, but something keeps telling you to keep the love you guys have and at least try to give it a chance. Darryl, if your wife was the one who killed someone or even if it were you, you wouldn't want to be loved any less. You wouldn't want people thinking any less of you. You wouldn't want to be alone. I know how that feels and it is not a good feeling. I was once that person who was alone and thought I would never come back from it. I am still not a hundred percent sure if I am okay and don't want to be the cause of my husband's fall."

Darryl put his hands on mine; he was looking at me and not saying anything. He just stared at me the whole time. He didn't apologize, didn't change the subject, but just stared at me. I wanted

to tell him to let go of my hands, but his were so warm. Darryl was

the type of guy who loved hard; he would say and do anything he

needed to do for the one he kept close to his heart. I noticed that he

had also been the same exact way with me since the day we met at

the hospital. I loved that he cared about me and how he always tried

to get my mind off of my problems but then bluntly telling me I

deserve better. I thanked God every day for him being in my life. If

Blake and I had never got together, I wonder if Darryl and I would

have ever met. Darryl and I had a good relationship, which was

strictly friendly. I knew if we both had the chance to date, we would

have probably been on vacation somewhere with our family, not

sitting there. For a while, we just watched a bunch of movies in

silence because our last conversation didn't go anywhere nor did we

decide to continue it. Sometimes I hated how we met and how we

sometimes only talked about my problems. Darryl knew more things

about me than I knew about him.

"Darryl, can I ask you a few questions?"

"Yeah, anything."

"Well it isn't exactly a question but tell me about yourself, your family, what you love, and why you chose your career."

"Well, I was born here in Atlanta, Georgia, and I resided here when my parents got a divorce. I was about to graduate high school. My parents loved me dearly. They would always try to put their differences behind them for me, but that didn't work out. I have a brother named Dashawn; he lives in California with his wife and three kids. I graduated from Howard University and was almost married, but she decided to leave me because I couldn't find work the first year out of college and a taxi gig wasn't enough for her. She thought I would give up on my career because I was bringing in a few hundred every night, but little did she know. I was always working on my career and wasn't going to settle. I will never forget what she told me a month before our wedding. She said, "Darryl you're broke, and I need a man with money. You will never become a psychiatrist." After that, I took what she said and ended up getting a job working for Dr. Landry. He saw potential in me and offered

227

me a job with an experienced paycheck. I love what I do. I love

helping people. I love music, reading, and just living life. I don't

believe you can live a good, happy, successful life without doing the

things you love and enjoy. I plan on marrying a woman that is just

like me in certain areas but also someone who is completely my

opposite. I want to have children and someday move down south and

retire. Now Janelle, I only know your broken story. Tell me

something else about you."

"I'll try but I am pretty broken and so is my life. I was born

here and both of my parents died on a plane crash. My brother and I

had been living with my grandparents. Ever since finding out that

my brother was killed, giving birth to my son, and being in a mental

institution, I haven't really talked to them. I just can't seem to pick

up the phone. I was a nerdy girl in high school. I loved school; I

graduated Valedictorian of my class. I also attended Howard

University with the major in business and law. I am one semester

from graduating with my master's in Law and two semesters of business. I planned on going back, but my life got in the way, and I haven't been back yet. Before I stopped working, I was working in a hospital as an LPN because I took a trade school class in high school. I was an overachiever. When I love, I love hard. I will not leave someone I love in the cold, and I could never not be a friend to someone. My love runs deep for everyone. I wear my heart on my sleeves, and people take that for granted. I am not used to failing, and now I am lost and don't know where to go or what to do. I am stuck and it's hard to breathe; I am drowning."

"I can save you, Janelle. Let me help you."

"No Darryl, I cannot just leave my husband. I know he didn't do me right, and I shouldn't be so understanding, but he is still my husband. I love him. I just can't do that right now.''

"I am not asking you to leave him right now. I understand, and I am not rushing you into anything you don't want, but I want you to know that I am here for you. I love you."

I couldn't understand why he told me that. Did he think it was going to cause me to forget my existing life and run off with him? I wish he wouldn't have told me that. That wasn't something I wanted to hear at that moment.

"Darryl please take me home."

I was reaching for my shoes trying to walk to the door, and Darryl was still sitting on the sofa. He wasn't even looking at me. Maybe he didn't hear me, or he was ignoring me. At that moment, I felt small. I felt like my feelings didn't matter. He was only thinking of himself by telling me he loved me and all of that other nonsense. I knew it was a bad idea when he reached out to me asking to hang out. I should have stayed at home in the bed, lying there feeling sorry for myself. I knew I shouldn't have been there because I was married and Blake did need my support, but I was so angry with him. I needed payback. I needed him to feel what I was feeling. I needed him to know that I didn't need him. However, at that moment, all I wanted to do was sleep in the bed with him while he woke up in the middle of the night and spooned me.

"Darryl take me home. I want to go home right now."

"Janelle why?"

"Why do I have to have a reason why I want to go home?"

"Do not answer my question with a question."

"And why not because the last time I checked, I could willingly speak on behalf of myself. I can say what I want to say. I am asking you to take me home, and you are refusing to do so. I don't understand why you won't."

"I don't want to take you home because now that I am telling you how I feel, you feel threatened or something. You are running from me when you should be running from your husband, but *love is pain.* Right?''

"That is not it. I need to go home. And what should I feel about someone who just openly confessed his love to a married woman? Is it something I should trust? No, it isn't because *love is pain*, but maybe it's all because it's me not wanting to hurt someone. I am a mess, and I don't want to mess you up. I like you Darryl, but I cannot turn you into a monster. I create monsters."

"Janelle, come here."

"No, please take me home."

"Janelle, I am not taking you home. Sit back on the couch. You don't need to leave the way you are feeling right now."

"Darryl, I can't be here with you, I need to be alone. I don't want to talk about any of this."

"Janelle, you have to talk about this. This is what's happening right now."

"I don't want to talk about leaving my husband or even about us. It's too much."

"Then we won't; we'll talk about something else. I just don't want you to go home right now. You just got here."

As I was removing my shoes, Darryl was getting up and coming over to me. He put his hand on my cheek. We were both staring at each other for a while when I kissed him. I could smell the strong cologne he was wearing, the smoothness of his hands against

232

my face. Our breathing was getting heavier as we kissed. Darryl

pushed me up against the wall by the steps and picked me up by the

legs, holding me up while we both passionately kissed each other.

My heart beat faster when we both looked up and kissed again. He

then walked me up the steps of his house and into his bedroom. He

lay me down on his king sized bed. The black comforter was soft

and smelled like it had been freshly washed and dried by God

himself.

Chapter 23

Darryl and I drove back to my place in silence. Nothing seemed to be on my mind except the fact that we had sex and it was better than being with Blake. I didn't know if it was because Blake was the only guy I have ever been with, but boy did I notice a huge difference. I wanted to stay in bed afterward and just cuddle with Darryl, but Blake kept on calling and texting me. I wanted to text him back to hurt him and tell him that I was enjoying my time away from him and was being satisfied in ways that he could fulfill. Going to Blake was the last thing I had wanted to do. I wanted to spend the night with Darryl, leave all of my problems and focus on myself. I wanted to have better sex with someone else and be happy, free, and comfortable.

I could tell Blake was still in the house because something was cooking. The house had an aroma that I hadn't smelled in a long time. Blake was preparing one of my favorite meals. Whenever I smelled garlic, I knew he was making his mom's homemade garlic bread, so I knew that he was cooking his homemade sauce to go with the shrimp, chicken, and garlic pasta. The first time Blake and I moved in with each other; he made that for dinner. Whenever he was in a bad mood or was sorry for something he had made me angry about, he would cook that dish. It was his way of apologizing because Blake knew that I wouldn't stay mad for long. I appreciated the thought that he put into preparing the meal for me, but I wasn't going to forgive so easily. He murdered my brother. Jean was my only sibling; we were so close. Jean was going to get married and have kids; he had a great life going for him. For his life to end the way it did, I would never get over it. It would stick with me forever.

Walking into the dining room, I took off my shoes and sat my keys on the glass table. Blake had the table set up for two and had the wine in ice. He hadn't lit the candles yet. I picked up the bottle of wine and poured me a glass. Blake wasn't in the kitchen, and the sauce smelled like it was burning. I turned the stove down and tasted it. The sauce was delicious. I couldn't wait to eat because I hadn't eaten anything before leaving earlier. I took a sip of the wine and sat back down at the table. I wondered where Blake was and what he was doing. While checking a few emails and social media, I came across an email from the detective that tried to arrest Blake a few days before. The email explained that they were still looking for him and if I knew of Blake's whereabouts, I would be held accountable as well. I knew that was going to happen eventually, but I figured they would have caught Blake, and I would be home not having to worry about it so much. The email began to talk about legal arrangements and murder charges, how it would affect me more than it would affect Blake. He continued by informing me of the consequences of harboring a fugitive. If I were caught, I would be thrown in jail. I wouldn't be able to see my son and my record would have a huge impact on my life.

I waited for Blake to come downstairs. He had not finished making the sauce. I didn't know what he was doing up there, but I hoped he wasn't trying to do anything romantic because I would refuse to have sex with him again. I was hurting, and as far as I was concerned, he should have been keeping that in mind. Blake could sometimes be the guy who wanted what he wanted and wouldn't stop until he got it. I wasn't sure what he wanted from me, but I did know that he was not getting it as long as I was angry with him. I was walking upstairs when Blake came running down the steps. He was wearing dark blue jeans and a black and white button-up shirt. He didn't realize I was home because he looked up at me with a puzzled expression. He looked like he wasn't expecting for me to be walking around my own house.

"Janelle, oh your home early."

"Yeah, I wanted to come home."

"He didn't try anything slick?"

"No, he didn't, I just wanted to be home."

"You guys had sex? I can see it on your face."

"What are you talking about? No, we didn't."

"Yes, you did Nells, you don't have to lie to me."

"I'm not lying.''

"Nells, just be honest, was he better than me?"

"Yes, he was. It was great actually!" Blake looked straight at me and then continued down the steps and into the kitchen. I knew I shouldn't have said that but he needed to feel like me. He needed to be hurt the way I was hurting.

"Janelle, I made you dinner. Are you going to eat with me?"

"If you want me too."

"So come into the dining room."

"Are you sure you want me to eat with you.''

"You are my wife, so why not?"

"Because I had sex with someone else."

"And I murdered you brother, you're still here with me, so how could I be mad."

I was about to answer Blake when someone broke the door down. I was in mid-sentence when police officers were running in the house. I was quickly grabbed and pushed up against a wall while the officer was putting handcuffs on me. Two other officers slammed Blake on the floor and started reading him rights. When Blake was able to see my face, he whispered, "I'm sorry, I love you." I looked at him and said, "I love you back," trying to fight back the tears. As I was being escorted to the police car, I saw the detective on the right side of the house smiling. He was staring at me shaking his head. I knew that I was going to get caught eventually, but I thought I would be able to get a little more time with my husband. Blake and I were put in the backseat of two different police cars. They were taking us both to the precinct downtown.

Driving downtown was mind blowing because I had to listen to the officer's talk about my husband. They talked about how he had to be mentally off to kill his own wife's brother. They talked about how he was sick to do what he did to me. I overheard the officer's partner whisper how I was stupid for allowing him to be in my home and not turn him in. The whole way, they shared their versions of the story they heard and the stories someone else had told them. Some of the things were true, but most of them were lies.

I slid down on the seat and started crying. I was about to be put in jail for not turning in a murderer and wasn't going to be able to see my son anytime soon if they didn't allow me to go free. I didn't want to be locked up, and I felt like I shouldn't have even been charged for anything because it was part of my brother's case. I only thought that I would find out the name Jean's killer and finally be at peace. Having to go up on the stand and be accused for his murder or even having to testify against my husband wasn't going to be easy. I didn't want to send him to jail because I didn't want Blake to not be able to see his son. He deserved to see him. Blake and Junior deserved to be together. I wanted nothing but the best for my son, and once again I was letting him down. He was with his aunt, and I was being thrown in jail, and so was his father. Junior was going to have a hard enough life without a man figure. He would also have to be without his birth mother as well. I knew I shouldn't have given birth; I should have had an abortion when I had

the chance to. You never think about the possibilities of your child's

life before you have them. You expect everything to go as planned

and for them to grow up and be great people. You never think about

your kid being a killer, a rapist, or even lonely because of your

actions. You think about them being a little like you or even like

their father. You try your best to teach them the right way to go in

life. You even teach them to be the best them they can be. You try so

hard to keep them protected that you eventually get caught up in that

and they end up being the opposite of what you wanted them to be. I

was one of those parents where I spent most of my days trying to

keep my family perfect. I actually let it get to the worse place

possible.

My lawyer was sitting in front of me writing down some

notes and looking for papers for me to sign. I watched him pull out

his phone and call a few people. He was a white guy with blue eyes

and blonde hair. He was the son of my original lawyer, but he died

and past on his law firm to him. His father would have asked me the questions he needed about fifteen minutes ago. His son took his time. He made sure he had everything he needed to back himself up and to make sure he had told his connections everything just in case he needed to get more information on the case. After about ten more minutes of my lawyer being on the phone, I noticed that he had a booger hanging out of his nose. I reached my hand out to tell him, but as soon as my hand went in the air, he picked the booger and flung it onto the floor. When I looked up at him, he smiled and wiped his hand on his pants. He went back to talking on the phone like he hadn't just picked his nose. I couldn't believe what I had witnessed. I thought he would use the tissues in front of him because he was around a female, or better yet, his client. He was doing a lot of talking to someone from his office and was holding up all of the time we had in the room. He had to also see Blake after we were done. He needed to talk to Blake about the money he had left us and everything else he had planned to do for us while he was in jail. It had become more complicated because I was being committed as well. Blake needed to set up an account for Junior to have once he turned eighteen if the both of us weren't able to provide for him before that time. I knew he was going to be locked up for a while because of the murder. I didn't know if Doctor Landry confessed to anything else.

"Okay, so the courts are saying they want to give you a few years because you were hiding your husband in your house while he was wanted. I am trying to come up with something that can maybe stray the judge from charging you with anything. It will be hard Janelle, but I am not saying it is not possible. I need you to tell me everything that happened."

"Okay I will, what do you need to know."

"Did you always know that your husband killed your brother?"

"No, but in the beginning, I did have my suspicions until the detective told me that it was a female that killed him."

"Were you aware of any changes in your husband and your brother?"

"No, they were best friends before we even started dating."

"So why did they stop being friends?"

"Blake said it was over a fight they had awhile back."

"Did he tell you about the fight?"

"I believe so, but I can't remember."

"How long have you and Blake been married?"

"We've been married for three years tomorrow, and we've been together for six in total."

"How was the marriage? Any huge fights? Abuse?"

"No, Blake would never lay a finger on me, he does have a temper, but he has never hit me. The marriage is fine, a few ups and downs but nothing we couldn't handle."

"How old is your son now?"

"He's almost one."

"Since you guys both might be in jail, who will have temporary custody of him?"

"I don't know. I will have to talk to Blake about who we want to take care of him. We only have his sister and my cousin that lives out here. I dont want to bring my grandparents into this because they were still mourning Jean and this would nearly kill them if they were to find out."

"Okay, once we are done, I will see if we can all sit together and work out those arrangements. Where is he now?"

"He's with Blake's sister."

"Okay, that's good. I'll be right back; I'm going to see if I can go and get Blake."

When he came back into the room, he had a look on his face that didn't look like he had good news. I sat there staring at him until he had gotten the courage to open his mouth about my husband. I could see he was trying to come up with something to say, but he was having a hard time.

"Janelle, I'm sorry, they already took Blake off to prison. He was sent on the bus about twenty minutes ago."

"Really? Okay, well can I make a phone call to see if someone would be able to keep my son? I really don't want him in foster care."

"Yes, you can use my phone."

"Thank you."

"No problem, I'll give you some privacy."

When my lawyer closed the door, I could hear him screaming at someone about how I had some important phone calls to make. They didn't want me calling anyone, and they were tired of waiting for me. I finally picked up his phone and started calling Blake's sister. I didn't know what I was going to say or if Blake already told her about what happened. I wasn't ready to leave my son behind again. I was feeling like I had lost in life and that my purpose wasn't even worth finding any more. I needed my husband. After the three rings, she finally picked up the phone. I could hear

Junior playing on the other end. He sounded so happy; she was

laughing when she answered the phone. I could tell that Blake hadn't

told her anything. I couldn't believe that I had to tell his sister how

he murdered my brother and was off to prison and I was going too.

"Hello.''

"Hey, it's me."

"Nelly?"

"Yeah, I have something to tell you and a huge favor to ask. I

need you to listen to every word I say."

"What is it?''

"Blake killed my brother Jean, and he got caught. Now he's

on his way to prison. I don't have a personality disorder; your

brother drugged me. The pills caused me to act that way because he

wanted to blame me for murdering my own brother. I knew what

was going on for a while. We didn't tell you earlier because I didn't

know all of the details, and Blake was missing in action. I just found

out exactly why he killed him and why he tried to blame me."

247

"Oh my god Nelly, are you okay? Where are you? Do you need some company?"

"No … I'm going to jail too. When they arrested Blake, we were in the house together. They are charging me for hiding a fugitive and whatever else they want to charge me with. I need you to keep Junior for a while. If you can't, I can ask my cousin, but since he's with you now, I figured that you might not mind."

"Nelly, of course I will keep him. How long do you guys have?"

"Well, I'm assuming that Blake has life or at least 25 years or something. My lawyer didn't tell me yet; he was letting me call about finding temporary childcare for Junior. Thank you so much, I really do appreciate this.''

"Your welcome girl. I love you.''

"Bye."

Chapter 24

I headed over to the water cooler in the corner of the room and took a cup out of the plastic wrapping. The button to the cooler was worn out where it would have said cold or hot. Pushing the button on the cooler for cold water, I could hear my lawyer talking to someone. I couldn't recognize the voice, but there was something familiar about it. That person's voice was deep and didn't sound like he was a lawyer or a police officer because I could tell my lawyer was trying his best to break down some of the things they were talking about. When I realized that I was going to be there a little longer than I thought, I paced the room. That was going to be the last time I wore regular clothes, got my hair done or even have natural hair products. Remembering how hard it was to be in a mental institution, I knew right then that I had finally hit rock bottom. I was losing my son, my husband, my life, and myself. That was the last day I would live a normal life before having to start repairing it for the better all over again. I couldn't tell if I was ever going to see the light at the end of the tunnel, but I did know my life wasn't going to end in that place, and I had to make the best of it, even though that was not what I had planned.

The water was warm and tasted like it was from the tap. It didn't have a fresh taste. What was worse, the cup was so cheap that the water was leaking from the bottom. I walked over to the trash can by the door and it inside. My lawyer knocked once on the door and then came into the room with a familiar face. I looked up and swore I saw my brother, but when I really took a closer look, it was someone else. I didn't know whether or not I should have been excited to see them, but I did smile and nodded when they asked me how I was doing. I hated those people who asked you how you were doing when they knew your situation. I was going to jail; I didn't think I would be excited to go there at almost midnight. My lawyer motioned for me to come and sit at the table with them. I walked over, and I could see that my attorney was ready to go home. He had taken off his suit jacket, and his tie was no longer around his neck. It was folded up inside his white button up front pockets.

For a minute, I was looking at the person next to him. He was talking about how he could get the lawyer to drop my sentence, but I would have to spend a lot of time on probation and going to parenting classes before I could have visits with my son. Also, they would allow me to visit my husband once they really understood my side of the story or if Blake confessed. I wanted nothing but to be able to go home and sleep knowing that I wasn't going to have to worry about my husband. I wanted to go home and enjoy the rest of my life.

Chapter 25

One day I was folding the inmate's clothes when one of the guards called me over and handed me some mail that I had received. I grabbed the letter from the guard's hand. She had a really bad attitude; we never got along. She reminded me of one of the girls who I wouldn't like in high school because she always thought that she was better than everyone else. She had that vibe about her, and I hated her for that. Once I took my mail, I heard her say something under her breath, but I ignored her and went back to folding clothes. One of the letters were from my cousin, which was always money or a short note of her telling me how much she loved me and how she was trying her best to get me out of there. Every few days, I would get a letter from Blake's sister sending me pictures of Junior and letting me know how he was doing. Sometimes she would send letters apologizing for her brother's mistake and how she didn't want to get in the middle of what happened. Blake's sister was a

wonderful person, and sometimes she acted as if she really liked me.
However, I knew that no matter what her brother did, she would
always side with him. I hated that about her because if he had
murdered me, she would take his side and be on the stand lying,
repeating whatever her brother told her to say. Even though she
would side with her brother, I knew she would keep her only
nephew safe and wouldn't harm him. She was honestly the only one
I knew who would take the best care of him. My cousin was great,
but that kind of environment wouldn't be good for my son to grow
up. The next letter was from Blake. He started sending me huge
packages or letters. I never opened any of them because I was so
angry with him. Yes, I did love my husband, but what we were
going through, I couldn't bear to open up and forgive him. When my
grandmother and I would go out for lunch, she would always tell me
that I needed to be more like my mother, which I hardly remembered
due to her life being cut short. She would say that my mom was such
a great woman, and even at my age, I was more like my father. My
grandmother hated that about me, but I loved it. The last time she

and I were together, she told me that love conquers all and without love there would not be a marriage. A marriage isn't just a letter, a ring, a church, or two people. She would say, "Girl marriage isn't about those tangible things, honey. When your marriage starts falling from the sky and your falling with it; don't forget to use the parachute." She always made it clear that neither Blake nor I should forget what would keep us from hitting the rocks at the bottom. When I had first gotten married, I didn't understand what she meant, but at that moment, our marriage was indeed falling from the sky and I wasn't using the parachute. I was watching myself take my life. I was watching the sky, the birds; I was taking too much time thinking about how my life was over instead of pulling the string that would keep me alive. I believe she meant love was our parachute. I think she was trying to tell me that I needed to be awake and stop dreaming. As I thought back on her wisdom, it made a lot more sense as I was actually going through the struggle that I didn't understand.

I folded the letters that I had sitting on a sticky metal table and put them into the side pocket of my jumpsuit. As I was folding the rest of the clothes, one of the other girls brought over two more carts and whispered in my ear. She carefully leaned in close to me. At first, I was a little skeptical, but when I heard what she said, I was a little easier. Every Tuesday, one of my roommates would get packages that wouldn't make it through security, so she paid off one of the guards to bring in her package through the back and into the laundry room. It would be sent to me; she usually had snacks for me or sometimes money. That was the worst thing I could get involved in, but I knew if I was going to last, I needed to make friends with them and start getting what I needed. I often thought about writing Blake and having him send me some things, but I never actually sent any of the letters I wrote to him. My shift was almost over, and I had to bring up the clean clothes to the rest of the ladies. I had to make sure none of the guards had seen me put the package in between the clothes. Once I got up to our cell, I had to hand the girl her clothes but also secretly hand off something she would give me to another inmate. It was one of the most annoying things I had to do, but I needed to make friends and make a name for myself if I was going to be there for a while.

I walked over to the same spot biting my nails so that the red-headed girl with freckles would see me. Every time she would come over, we would have the longest conversation because she only talked to a few black women there and was clearly excited to have black friends. She was the type of white girl who needed to have African American friends to prove to her family that she knew people who grew up in the hood, and she could make it anywhere if she just got a taste of a black person in her life. She was so weird, but I needed her to get the task done. As we talked about her family, I was more focused on what was in the current letter that Blake had sent. It was a lot heavier than the last few. I really wanted to know about his case. I wanted to know if he had gotten out of jail and was spending time with our son, or was he at home living the life he always wanted. Just thinking about him at home in our bed relaxing while I was there for his stupid crime made me even angrier. I knew the type of man Blake was. If he could do what he did to me, I knew

he was capable of getting himself out of jail. At that point, I wasn't

even hearing what the white girl was saying. I was angry; I was

nearly in tears not wanting to bust out crying and cursing. I had to

hold myself together at least until I got back to my room. I stared at

the girl letting her know that I wasn't in the mood to talk anymore.

She leaned in and grabbed my butt; she inserted the envelope into

my side pocket and quickly walked away. I waited for a few seconds

and then made my way to my room. When I got there, my roommate

was sitting on her bed reading one of those boring romance novels

that only had fine white men on the cover with their shirts off

coming out of the water at the beach. I hated those books; I always

thought they were such a joke.

"I'm glad you made it back, I was wondering if you had

gotten caught or something. I was just about to come and find you."

"Nope, I got it. You know that white girl can talk forever."

"Yeah I know, she can. So where is the envelope?"

"Oh yeah, here."

"Thanks girl, here's your twenty bucks. Nice doing business with you."

Putting away the money that I had just made, I pulled out the two envelopes that I had gotten earlier. I noticed that the one Blake had written to me was not addressed from the same place as the others. It was a different address, to be correct it wasn't even addressed from a prison. It had a regular home address. I was almost crying just thinking that he had gotten out before me. I opened up the envelope and pulled out the papers that were inside. When I opened the letter, the top of it said, "Baby I love you, and I am going to get you home soon. Please be patient." I continued reading, and Blake stated that he was released because he had someone pay his bail. The judge was someone who knew him from college and owed him a huge favor. He was an old college friend that I met the night of our wedding. He was a close friend of Blake's, but I didn't know anything else about him. I didn't even know he went to school for law or was a damn judge. I felt like there were so many people that Blake knew but I didn't.

The rest of the letter stated that the judge sentenced him to a few months like me, but he got out for good behavior. He said that he had spoken to my lawyer and that I would have to stay a little longer because he was yet to go to court. He also said that we would have a private case, and no one would have to appear for jury duty. Whatever the judge decided, the case would be settled. To be honest, none of it made any sense because it was going against everything right. The judge was going to let us off easy, and Blake would be set free of being a murderer. I would have to live with that for the rest of my life. The end of the letter said that he was so upset that I hadn't written him back months ago. He thought that since I loved him, I wouldn't ignore him. Finally, he stated that he would like for me to respond with something after reading that letter.

It was a lot to think about. I couldn't believe that I was going to get out of jail soon, and hopefully would be able to see my son and grandparents. I had missed them so much. After going through

all of that, I wouldn't have traded my family for the world.

Chapter 26

After waiting for my husband to get his lawyer to get me out of jail, I was finally leaving. I was so excited. My husband once again saved me. I don't know what he did or how he did it, but I was so happy. I was a little nervous to be going home and having to start over once again, but I would have to get over it and just make the best of everything. Things could have been worse; I could have been killed or beat up in that place. If it weren't for my roommate letting me help her out, I would have been so lost. I would have probably survived with my husband's help, but when I first arrived, I was so upset and angry with him. Nothing he said would change the fact that he had killed my brother. I still didn't understand why he killed him and would do what he had done to me, but I did know that he would always save me. He always kept me safe whenever I was in trouble. Blake would do anything for me. After learning his true colors, I would not be getting myself too close to him. I did love my husband, but I couldn't allow myself to trust him fully.

The bed that I was lying on was hard and cold. No matter how long I had been there, I still couldn't get used to it. It was like lying on rocks in the middle of January. I couldn't wait to get out. On my last day, my roommate was supposed to get all of us girls together to have a going home party. My roommate was nice, but I had a feeling she wanted to throw that party for herself because she was leaving a few days after me. She had been there for four years for something she never wanted to tell me about. I always wondered what she had done, but she never told anyone. She was so private about her life. The only thing that I did know was that she had two older sons. They were both in high school and lived with her younger sister back in Missouri. She had been talking about going to see her kids. She seemed like a great mother. If she weren't going back to Missouri, I would've loved for us to be friends because she was the only one that I was able to somewhat build a connection with. I was going to miss her.

"Janelle, aren't you so glad that you're finally getting out of here?"

"Yes I am, I can't wait to take a nice hot bath and to get a massage."

"Girl me too, right after I spend some time with my kids, I am taking my little ass straight to the spa because four years in here has not been good to me at all."

"Yeah, I can imagine. I've only been here for a few months, and I am already having back problems."

"Girl that ain't nothing, but I'm so glad that your leaving. You are too good for this place."

"Yeah."

"Hey, Janelle."

"Yes, girl?"

"Can I ask you what you're going to do once you go back to your husband? Aren't you afraid to be home alone with him?"

263

"I haven't been thinking about him or what he might do to me when I get home. The only thing that I have been thinking about is how angry I am with him for what he has put me through and how in love I am with him at the same time. The whole time that I have been here I've been trying to fall out of love, which is crazy because my whole life is Blake. You know what I mean?"

"Yes, I get exactly what you mean because when my ex-husband cheated on me twice, I took him back and was happy playing step mommy to his new kids. I was there helping him raise them until I ended up here and got divorced. Sometimes you have to think about what life would be without him, how you could survive, and how much your kid needs him in his life. It's hard raising boys to become men when they don't have a male figure in their lives. It's way harder when you resent their father when your kids only want you to love him."

My roommate got up from her bed and walked over to her cabinet at the end of the bed and was pulling everything out. Her blonde hair was in a long French braid. She always kept it braided.

She never left it out. That was strange because white women loved having their hair out. I watched her dig through all of her belongings, which she never went through. When she finally finished pulling everything out, she came over to my bed and sat next to me. She had a few letters and a few pictures in her hand, but the first thing she did was unfold a dirty piece of paper which looked to be a newspaper article. I could tell that she was nervous about showing me, so I didn't say a word to her. I just laid in the same spot. She just kept looking at the paper breathing in and out. She was shaking, and her hands couldn't keep still. She was scratching her hands when she finally got the courage to show me the paper. At first, I didn't know what I was looking at. It was a newspaper article from four years prior. The headline said *The New Bonny & Clyde of Missouri.* The rest of the paper stated that they had robbed over fifteen banks in their city and had never got caught until my roommate turned herself in. It also stated that there was no trace of her husband and that their children were found home alone that night. The children were not aware of their parent's robberies, and they were left to live with a relative. By the time I got to the bottom

of the article, it had their pictures. My roommate was wearing a red

baseball cap with a black hoodie, and her husband was dressed in a

white button-up shirt with black jeans. After the picture, it stated

that she was supposed to get fifteen years and would never be able to

get custody of her sons and wouldn't ever get a job. I couldn't

believe that she was hiding that from everyone. The crime she

committed wasn't that bad, but I guess to her it was an

embarrassment.

"Stacey you didn't have to hide this from me, I wouldn't

have thought anything less of you."

"I knew you wouldn't, but I've been trying to hide the fact

that I did this. I did all of this for my husband, but I had to turn

myself in because he threatened to take my kids away once I found

out that he had another family and had me committing crimes for

them."

"Stacey girl, you were stupid in love, and we all make

mistakes, so stop being so hard on yourself."

"I'm so glad I told you this because I really needed to tell someone. I was getting tired of keeping secrets from you."

"Well, I am glad you felt like you needed to share the truth with me."

She hugged me so tight I thought I was going to stop breathing. But to be honest, I hadn't been embraced by anyone in such a long time. It felt good to be hugged by someone else other than my husband. It was getting late, and I was on my way to the cafeteria to eat dinner when one of the guards said that I had a phone call waiting for me in the conference room. I never got phone calls, so I didn't know who was calling me and inmates were only able to use the phone in there if you asked and if the guard who was in there liked us or got something in return. I knew it wasn't going to be my cousin or grandparents because they never called or wanted to be called. They always wanted to write letters. Everyone knew I was going home the next day, so It had to be my lawyer. Walking down the dark hall to the conference room, I noticed the girls lined up talking and waiting to get their medications cr feminine products.

Everyone was talking to someone. They all looked tired and hungry as if they hadn't slept in days. The only girl I knew was the one who was seven months pregnant. I was familiar with her because I had helped her when one of the other ladies were trying to fight her over her food that was sent there for her. The girl was young; she had to be at least eighteen years old. She was the baby, so everyone tried to take advantage of her.

As I was reaching the conference room, I could hear one of the guards screaming that they needed me to hurry up. I kept hearing him say my name. I knew exactly who he was because he tried to get me to have sex with on my first day there, and I refused. He had gotten me in trouble that night, and I ended up being put in one of the isolation rooms. It was the worst first night I could have ever experienced. When I walked in, Darryl was sitting in one of the chairs. I stopped in the doorway staring. He got up from the table, and I noticed that he was wearing a denim button up shirt with denim jeans; he had the bottoms rolled up a little so I could see his ankles, and he had white Vans on. I always loved the way he dressed. I could tell that he took the time to dress whenever he was going out. I couldn't believe that he was there; I hadn't talked to him since the night I was arrested. He was there when I was handling a bunch of things for Junior that night with my lawyer. That was the last time I saw him and thought about him. I thought that maybe he gave up trying. I walked over to Darryl, and we both grabbed each other and held each other for what felt like five minutes. I couldn't believe that someone I barely knew would come to see me and my own husband wouldn't. I sat down and watched Darryl motion for the guard to leave the room. I was shocked to see that he had listened to him because that man really hated me and would do anything to make my life a living hell. I watched Darryl dig through his bag for some papers. He wasn't saying anything to me; he was just grabbing papers and flipping through white pages.

"What are you looking for, Darryl?"

"I wrote you a bunch of letters, but I never sent them, and I brought them to give to you."

"What do you mean? You came all the way up here for that?" Darryl was still fumbling through his bag trying to get the rest of the letters. He was sighing the whole time. He was acting very strange.

"Darryl, please sit down."

"No Nelly, I have to find this letter. It's really important that I find it."

"Darryl, please stop looking. Just tell me." He kept on looking through his bag. I got up to grab his arm when he sat down and looked up at the ceiling. I didn't know what was wrong with him and why he was acting so strange, or why he had come all the way up there over some letters that he wrote.

"Nell's, please listen to me! I've been thinking about you none stop since the day I saw how bothered you were when you left my house. After about an hour, I called you a few times, and I didn't get an answer, so I kept calling until something didn't feel right. I went over to your house, and one of the neighbors was outside. I asked them if they had seen you and they told me that you and Blake were arrested. I rushed over to county, pretended to be your psychologist, and got to speak to your lawyer. I was so worried about you. I was out there trying to get your lawyer to let me pay your bail, but he said that you had to go to prison and no one was able to pay the bond at that time. When I saw you sitting in that room, it hurt me to see you in so much pain. You looked as if you were done fighting, like you were done loving and not anyone else but yourself. You were not the same woman I met back at Doctor Landry's facility." Daryl looked away and at the ground. He didn't say anything else; he just kept his eyes low. I leaned closer to him and touched his face; it was soft and warm. I felt his beard; I never thought he could pull off a beard. I played with it for a few seconds. Then he looked up at me and had tears in his eyes. I never saw him that way before. I knew he had feelings for me, but until then, I never knew he cared so much.

"Darryl, I need you to understand; I am married. Yes, I like you, but you can't keep this up. I cannot ruin what I have with my

271

husband. I need him. He takes care of me, and I don't know anything outside of him. I hate that about myself, but right now is really not the time to be pouring your heart out to me."

"Do you here yourself Nell? You sound crazy. I need you to really think about what you just said. You sound like you were not anyone before your husband. I know you were raised better, not to be dependent on a man. You told me that you had a life outside of him even when you guys got married, so why do you now feel like that he's all you have?"

"Because he is getting me out of here just like when I was all alone in the hospital."

"He put you in all of these places, every place you should have not been to begin with." You cannot let this man take your life. You need to take it back. I want you to have better."

"So what? You can do better? You can love me better, take care of me better, and provide for me better. I get that but why should I be listening to you anyway?"

272

"You are wrong; we both were together on my bed. We both wanted it, and you can't even sit here and act like you didn't. I am not trying to hurt you or take you from someone you love and have built a life with, but I am trying to show you what you deserve. You need and deserve better than Blake. I'm sorry if this is too much for you, but this is why I came here. Your lawyer called me and told me that you were leaving tomorrow, so I took a chance on hope and came all the way out here for you. I want to help you, to show you what real love feels like. I want to show you that not every black man with a degree is dirty and does everything illegally."

"Darryl this is too much for me. I need time; I need to figure things out first. We can't just jump on our feelings, at the end of the day feelings turn into nothing. I can't be in my feelings for you and leave my husband when I have a child who needs us both, and the whole situation is complicated."

"Janelle." He touched my cheek, lifted up my head. He leaned in and kissed me. The last time we kissed had been some time ago. It felt good; it felt like home. It was like I had never left, and that was all a nightmare, and I was going to wake up. We stopped

kissing, I looked around and realized that I was still in that hellhole

sitting in a room with Darryl not knowing what I was going to do.

Blake was my husband; I loved him. Darryl showed me his heart; he

wanted me for me. I was stuck between two worlds that I wanted. I

wanted to spend the rest of my life with my high school lover,

someone who gave me everything I needed and wanted, but at the

same time, he caused me so much pain. And then the other side,

there was something new, fast and not secure. I was hearing battling

between two different goods. I needed to understand. I needed my

grandmother's advice. I needed to see her.

Chapter 27

I was finally awake and was alone in the room. I didn't know where Stacey had gone since it wasn't time for us to be awake. I didn't even hear her get out of the bed, which I usually do. It was so unreal that I was going home. It was another day where I was starting over. I hated starting over. Each time I started over, it ended worse. I was worse off each time I went back home. The more I thought about going home; I realized that I was going to have to face Blake. It had been so long since I last talked to him or even looked at him. I wondered if he still smiled the same. Did he age being in jail? Had he lost all attraction towards me? Blake was indeed my husband, but he was also a stranger. I remember the day we first met. It was way earlier before we dated. We were in the same Criminal Justice class. He was always on the opposite side of me during our debates. The teacher always made sure it was that way because, from the first day of class, she wanted to warm us up for our daily debates. She wanted us to get a feel of debates. If we couldn't handle the first day, she wanted us to drop the class before it was too late. So that day Blake and I happened to be picked to debate about people's sexuality. Boy, that was the worst thing to debate because Blake really enjoyed throwing huge curve balls at me. Whenever I was proving him wrong, he always had something else smarter to say. Ever since that day in class, we were close friends. I didn't know he was Jean's friend until one day at my brother's basketball game. After that day, we were even closer because my brother had nothing but good things to say about Blake. So he instantly stole my heart.

It was 6:00 a.m. and everyone was up and out of their room, and I was packing to leave. Blake was supposed to be there waiting for me, so I wasn't in a rush. That day seemed to be the most depressing day of them all because I was going home, and home was no longer a home. Blake and I weren't as connected; my son was growing up without me. I was still unemployed, my skin wasn't in any good condition, and I had lost a lot of weight. I was having serious issues, and wouldn't ask for help, so my body wasn't doing well because of that. I needed some happiness. I needed love. I needed a warm bed. I needed coconut oil. My life needed a good rub down.

Before I knew it, Blake was waiting for me in the guest room where we usually have visitors come. Blake was wearing a black V-neck shirt with a denim jean jacket; he had on some ugly gray sweat pants. I hated when he wore those unless it was "sweat pants" season, which it was, but at that moment, all sexual desires went out of the window. I didn't want him inside of me. I didn't even want him looking at me. Blake's face lit up when he saw me coming from the back. When he noticed that I didn't have a smile on my face, he dropped his. He looked a little confused as to why I wasn't happy like he had forgotten what he had done and gotten me into.

"Nelly, I missed you so much. Come here." I walked over to him sitting down in one of the orange chairs. He had an envelope on the table with him. It didn't have any writing on it. It was blank. The letter looked like it had something inside. I stood in front of the table staring at him. Blake got up from behind the table and pulled me in

for a hug. I thought our hug would feel different. I thought it would

feel cold, and I would still be angry. But nope, it was warm,

comforting, and seemed like love. It felt the same as always. It

relaxed me. I was not hurting.

"Baby, are you ready to go? I bought you something to eat.

Are you hungry?"

"Yeah, I am. What did you get?"

"You know your favorite?"

"And what's that Blake?"

"A breakfast sandwich from the spot by your old house." He

smiled at me and lifted up a brown paper bag.

"Blake you didn't have to do that. But it's probably cold

now."

"No, I heated it up right before you came out. Here."

"Thank you." I didn't know what he was doing with the whole let me bring you something you love gesture. Things were still the same, and we still needed to talk about what we were going to do, how we were solving our issues.

As we were walking to the car, Blake grabbed my hand. His hands were cold; I could see his breath in the air. He was walking slow and pulled me behind him while he took us to where the car was parked. Blake wasn't any different than from the last time we were together. That night when we both got arrested, I still remembered how we were feeling towards each other. We were being childish, and now that we both were able to be free together, I needed us to get things fixed. I needed to know where we both stood. I knew I wanted to find trust again and to be able to forgive because of my son. I didn't know where Blake stood. Before, he wasn't trying to give up on us but wanted us to move past everything. He was aware of how I felt; he knew I wasn't ready and wasn't happy with him.

Blake pulled out his keys and opened the front door for me. He took my bag and put it in the back seat of the car. He waited for me to get in before he closed the door. I watched him through the mirrors as he made it to the other side of the car. Blake had driven my SUV; there were still things in the back of the car, which told me he hadn't cleaned anything. He probably hadn't cleaned the house from the last time we were there. I sat in the passenger's seat eating my food. The car was in total silence. We didn't talk for the first hour ride back home. Blake kept his eyes on the road; he didn't even pull out his phone when it was ringing. That had to be all too good because Blake was acting as if we were on our way back from a trip, were both happy, and had never been on that rollercoaster. A little part of me wanted to yell and scream at him, make him leave me right there, and even smack him upside his big ass head. I was feeling so many emotion's during that car ride.

As we drove towards home, I was thinking what it would be like. Blake and I were still married, I still had a son, and I still knew that Darryl had feelings for me, but the one thing that was different was my environment. Was I going home to the same place where it went downhill, or did Blake somehow move us somewhere else? Was I ever going to get a job? I didn't know what my future held going back home.

Blake stopped at a motel. It was getting dark out; the motel lights were on. I could see someone in the office window. It looked like they were on the phone. The rooms of the motel were mostly occupied. The lights were on in almost every room except for one at the end. It was dark in that area. The overhead lights must've blown out because the rest of the lights outside were on. I didn't know if Blake and I were going to stay there or not, but I needed to get out of the car. While I sat waiting to see what Blake was doing, I noticed him staring at me, so I turned around and faced him.

"Janelle, we need to talk."

"What about?"

"Us, our life. We are now heading home for good this time, and I don't think we should keep any more secrets from each other."

"Don't say we don't need to keep secrets from each other because the last time I checked, it was because of you. You are the reason we are even here in the first place."

"Nelly, I know and that's what we need to talk about. I don't want to get home and you're still angry at me."

"Do you even know what you're saying right now? You don't want me to be angry with you." I turned around to look out of the window. I couldn't believe what I was hearing. I really couldn't believe that he thought it was the both of our faults as to why we were sitting in the car upstate driving me from prison.

"Can we please talk Janelle? I really want to work this out." I hopped out of the car and walked over to the office. Blake was still in the car looking at me. He didn't move for a second. He was just looking. When I walked into the motel's office, the lady at the front desk was watching the news. She was so into it; she didn't even notice that anyone had walked in. I walked closer to the desk and thought she would have heard me, but she still had her eyes glued to the television screen.

"Excuse me, miss."

"Oh my god, you scared me."

"You really need to get a bell or something, I could have shot you, and you wouldn't even have seen it coming."

She looked at me funny. She wasn't sure if I really had a gun or not. The woman was staring at me until someone walked in behind me. I noticed she had jumped back. She looked frightened. When I turned around, I noticed it was just Blake. This lady was acting as if she had never seen black people before. I really couldn't wait to leave because the white people there were way too scary for me. They couldn't believe that black people existed. They probably only heard of us on the news. We were probably some unknown creature to them, which was horrible to say, but they really need to re-educate themselves about us. When I was growing up, white people were the ones killing their families, blowing up schools, and trying to kill presidents. It wasn't until one guy did some drugs and was on the news because the side effects weren't like any other. He was acting like he had lost his mind and people didn't know how else to respond. Ever since then, whites had totally become publicly racist and ignorant.

Blake was giving the lady his information and paying her for our stay. I didn't know how long we were staying, but I needed to sleep in a real bed and to take a nice bubble bath. I needed to feel comfortable for at least one night. I figured if one night could relax me, I would be able to keep sane until I was back home living with my issues. In the motel room, Blake and I immediately walked over to the bed and sat down. Blake looked tired; he was sitting there sighing. He didn't once look over at me. I lay down beside him. He was still sitting there. I lay on the bed while Blake was staring at the ground. I wondered what he was thinking about. I wasn't sure what he was feeling. That was the first time that we were not speaking to each other. We usually never went to bed angry. I couldn't even remember the last time Blake stopped talking to me. That was the first time I ever noticed him looking like he was tired and not full of life. I was watching Blake breathe softly. I could see his back rising every time he would inhale. For a minute, I didn't know if he would ever get up from that spot. He wasn't moving; he never even looked up from the ground. I wasn't sure if I should ask if he still wanted to talk or not because that was something new that I was seeing. Before I knew it, I was lying down drifting off to sleep. Before falling asleep, I remember Blake was still sitting on the bed looking at the ground. He had not once looked back at me, nor did he take off his jacket.

When I woke up from my nap, I noticed the sun was completely down and the blinds were still open, I could see people walking back and forth past the window. A few were carrying ice buckets back to their rooms. Some of them were laughing. It had to be about six of them outside. Someone out there said something about going out to the bar up the road and from then on they were loud. I wished they would leave; they were distracting. As soon as I got up from the bed to close the blinds, the people that were outside started walking down the street. They were heading out of the parking lot. I could see that they were drunk because one of the guys was carrying a bottle with them. When I turned around to face

Blake, he was walking out of the bathroom with a towel wrapped around his waist. He took it off, reached into a plastic bag, and took out a pair of black Calvin Klein boxer briefs. I watched him walk over to the front door. He grabbed the last few bags that were sitting there and threw them onto the bed. He never said a word. Blake went into one of the bags and took out a pair of white socks. I was sitting up on the bed wondering why he hadn't moved the rest of the bags. I got up, looked inside, and saw that there were panties, a few bras, socks, a pair of black and blue jeans, and a few white, black, and gray t-shirts.

He was staring up at the ceiling. I couldn't believe that he was lying there in complete silence after he had told me that he wanted to talk to me. I decided to walk over to the bed and get undressed. I was taking my clothes off, and Blake was still just lying there. I got on the bed and lay down next to him. Facing him, I leaned closer and softly put my hand on his shoulder. I wanted him to know that I was willing to talk, that I wasn't as mad and was prepared to understand and give him his time to explain what he was

286

thinking. Blake just lay there. At first, I was going to turn over and go back to sleep, but I wanted to see what was wrong with him. That wasn't usually the way Blake handled things with me. We always talked to each other because in the beginning of our marriage I wanted to go to bed angry, but one day we both were tired of not having sex on those nights. We then started scheduling sex nights because Blake always wanted to try "new" things with me. To be honest, it was the best thing we could have ever done because it kept us happy. We enjoyed those nights, which also made us communicate more.

Chapter 28

Blake and I were a great couple; we never seemed to have big issues in our marriage. We genuinely loved each other at one point. I believed that deep down I still loved Blake, but at that moment, sitting in that motel room, lying on the bed, staring at Blake while he ignored me, I wasn't so sure if I could still love him. After noticing that he had drifted off to sleep, I decided to go into the bathroom to take a shower.

About thirty minutes later, I was getting out of the shower. The clock's green numbers showed that it was only ten-thirty. Blake was still sleeping in the same spot on the bed. Staring at him, I wanted Blake to turn over and demand for us to have sex. I wanted him to have come up with some new spontaneous ideas of where and how we could have sex. I wanted Blake to grab my legs, lift them up in the air, and eat me out. I wanted my toes to curl. I wanted Blake to kiss me on the ass and make me come multiple times. The last time we had great sex was on Blake's birthday. We were in Jamaica. It was so hot outside. We both decided to go to the beach early that morning, and we had sex on the beach right at the foot of the shore. It was cool having the water hitting us. It was for sure different since we'd never done that back home. We both enjoyed ourselves. But Blake was just sleeping, not even facing me. How could he sleep at a time like this? I was horny, didn't know if I loved the man I was lying next too, if he loved me, or if we were ever going to talk like he had wanted too. At that moment, I knew that I was not in the right space to be there with him. I needed to get away; I needed someone to talk to about us. I couldn't talk to Blake because I would always get angry when we did try to talk. Talking to him about what happened always seemed to piss me off. It made me so angry to the point where I didn't want to be bothered. I wanted this whole situation to be over with. As I lay there staring at Blake sleeping, I wanted to wake him up and talk to him, have sex with him, something. It was so hard not to desire my husband.

While I was in deep thought, I noticed Blake waking up, so I turned around to face the other side of the room. Blake was getting up from the bed. I watched him walk into the bathroom. He didn't look back at me to see if I was sleeping or not. He just kept on walking. The bathroom light never came on; he was just peeing and then it stopped. When he came out, he stopped and looked over at me for what seemed like five minutes. He didn't say anything at first; we were both just staring at each other. I watched Blake walk back over to the bed. I watched him stare at me the whole time. I sat up and put my naked body under the covers. Blake sat on the bed and smiled at me.

"Blake are you okay?"

"Yes I am, can we talk now?"

"Sure."

I looked up at the ceiling trying to keep from crying. Blake had gotten back up and went over to his duffle bag and pulled out a pair of boxers and a black wife beater. He handed them to me. I took the clothes and put them on. The whole time I was getting dressed, Blake watched me. He watched my every move. He didn't say a word. He didn't move; he didn't even try anything. He just watched.

"So what do you want to talk about Blake?"

"Nell's, first I want to start off by saying I am sorry. I am sorry for betraying you; I am sorry for lying to you. I really didn't mean for all of this to go the way it did. I never meant to hurt you. I don't know why I killed your brother. I do know why I was angry at him, and it was stupid for me to hurt you the way that I did, and I am sorry." Blake was just staring at me; he didn't say anything else. I wasn't sure if he wanted me to say anything back. I had heard it all before; he had said that a hundred times. It was like watching a rerun of some boring ass sitcom that I hated, but Blake loved.

"Blake what do you want me to say. I am hurt, angry, and bitter. Yes, I love you, but then I don't. I think I hate you more because sometimes I just want to kill you and get revenge, but then other times I want to just straddle you and scream daddy at the top of my lungs. I am confused. I would have never imagined you as a

291

killer, someone who would hurt me. But you did, you did just that and for you to sit here and apologize again with the same line as the last time doesn't make me believe you. I can't believe you."

"Baby, I am so sorry. I want you to believe me. I want you to love me again. I know this is hard for you. I love you, and I mean that. I just had gotten caught up. I didn't mean for you to go down for this." I cut him off.

"What? You framed me, you drugged me, and put me in a mental institution and knew nothing was wrong with me. That was you. All of that was the plan of you. That is who you are and for me to be so stupid and not notice that is crazy. You don't understand how I feel, how my life is over. I can never go back to work; I can never have a good relationship with our son. He loves you; he knows you. You took that away from me. So right now I hate you." I got up from the bed and walked into the bathroom. I turned on the lights and started crying. I looked at myself in the mirror for the first time being out of prison and saw that my face had changed, I looked at myself really good. I didn't recognize me. I was different. I smirked.

"Baby I am truly sorry. I know you are not going to forgive me for a long time and you might not ever, but I need us to talk. I need us to get through this; I need you." Blake was walking into the bathroom. He walked in behind me. He put his hands on my shoulders. They were warm but rough. I moved away from him. I looked at him through the mirror and noticed that he was crying. His eyes were watery. Blake never usually cries. I had to stay strong. I didn't know if he was playing with me or if he was really sincere. I just didn't know.

"Blake please go sit back down, I'll be right out. I really just need a minute." As I watched Blake leave the bathroom, I turned on the faucet and splashed my face with some cold water. Reaching over to pick up the towel on the counter, I could hear Blake in the background fumbling through something. I was wondering what he was getting. Was he getting the weapon he used to kill my brother? Was he going to kill me? I wasn't sure what was going to happen to me, but I was for sure afraid. Blake was capable of a lot of things but was he capable of killing the love of his life, which I assumed I was.

Thinking about Blake murdering me was not what I wanted to think about, but what else could I think of. I was stupid for even getting in the car with him, accepting the food, walking into this motel room and even talking to him. I wouldn't know if he was going to snap or not. He was too calm to be angry, so I was unprepared for him, I was leaving myself open.

The next thing I knew Blake was on the phone talking to someone. He was answering the person on the other ends questions with yes and no's. He wasn't questioning the other person. Who would he be on the phone with? We were in the middle of discussing what we needed to get over, and he was on the phone handling some kind of business. Blake was always about work. He didn't leave his work at the office. Before we got there, I wouldn't question Blake about who he was talking too or what he was talking about, but at that moment, I needed to know who the hell he was talking too. What could have been more important than us? He was really handling work-related tasks during our talk. I know I walked away, but I needed a minute. I didn't need for him to forget about what we were doing and busy himself with his work.

The next morning Blake and I were headed out to get breakfast and then off to go shopping for a few things. It was around nine thirty in the morning. I waited in the car for him to get off the phone with a client when I saw a guy coming out of the fifth motel room. He was carrying a brown leather briefcase; it looked like it was brand new. He stood out to me because he was wearing a royal blue tailored suit with a purple button up shirt underneath. The shirt was unbuttoned at the top. He didn't have on a tie. His shoes were brown; they were men's Oxfords. Blake had a pair in the same exact color. This guy was handsome; he wasn't American. He had to be Pakistani or something. He looked foreign. His hair was pushed back with a side part. It wasn't gelled down, but I could tell he had something in it to keep it back. It was something light weight because his hair still moved as he walked. It wasn't long, it was at the top of his ears, jet black and gorgeous. This man had a well-groomed beard. It was cut short, full, and thick. On top of that he had a nice thick mustache as well. He had nice olive skin like he was just getting back from traveling. It was nice and even. His eyes were hazel; they were bright. I couldn't help but stare at him. Blake was nothing compared to him. Even though Blake was my Drake, this man was way better than either of them. I was staring at him so hard; I didn't notice him walking over to the truck. I sat up and straightened my hair. I made sure the curls that were dangling in my face were behind my ears. I licked my lips so that they didn't seem to be as dry as they were. I looked straight and acted like I wasn't staring at him and watched the owner of the hotel in the front. She was sweeping the porch. She was casually watching me while I looked at her and at the fine man walking up to my truck knowing he wasn't the man I came with. She was staring hard. I tried not to look over at the guy standing next to me. He leaned in and tapped on the window. I didn't have the keys to the truck, so I looked over and smiled. He motioned for me to roll the window down. He showed off his big bright, healthy teeth. I smiled at him and opened the door. When I got out of the car, I realized that he was tall, probably standing over six foot three. He happened to be a little taller than Blake. He stepped back a little bit and placed his briefcase on the ground. The ground was nothing but rocks and pebbles. I looked up at him, and he was still staring at me. I glanced behind him to see if Blake was coming out and of course he wasn't. He was probably still on the phone.

"Hi sir, can I help you?"

"Good morning to you too." He smirked.

"I'm sorry, good morning." I looked at him waiting for him to say something back.

"So how are you this morning? It's a beautiful morning."

"Yes it is, I'm fine. How are you?"

"I am blessed, Allah created this great day."

"Oh, are you Muslim?"

"Yes, I am. Does that bother you?"

"No, but why did you come over to my car?"

"Well, to be honest, I saw you staring at me, and I thought I should introduce myself."

"Oh, you did. Well, you still haven't introduced yourself."

"Your beauty distracted me."

"I am married."

"That won't stop me."

"Are you serious? You don't even know me."

"Are you happy?"

"Yes. Very."

"How many wives do you have?"

"Actually, I only have one. I have three children. They are back home in my country."

"So what are you doing in the U.S.?"

"Work."

"And what do you do for a living?" I waited for him to answer. He stopped and stared at me. He didn't give me an answer. He stood there staring, smiling, showing off those beautiful white teeth. I smiled back; the man had game. He used his charm so well; he knew how to play the game. He knew just what to say and how to say it.

"My names Janelle. Yours?" I extended my hand for a handshake. He grabbed my hand and kissed it. I pulled it back. He smiled.

"My name is Saif Abdullah. Janelle is a beautiful name. Where are you from?"

"I am American. My parents are from Ghana."

"I've never met an African woman as beautiful as you."

"Saif, please I am married. I appreciate the compliments, but this is not appropriate."

"I am just complimenting you. I will stop if this is uncomfortable."

"It's not uncomfortable because I am married, it's uncomfortable because you're married with three kids in your country."

"In my homeland, we are allowed to marry more than one woman. We could get married, and since you're not happy in your marriage, you can become my wife. I will give you exactly what you deserve."

"What makes you think I am not happy? What makes you think that I find you attractive? And what makes you think I date out of my race?"

"Well, you were staring at me as I was walking to my car that made you seem interested. And don't ever judge a book by its cover. Just because I am not the same race as you doesn't mean I can't treat and please you the way you deserve to be. Race has nothing to do with how people treat you. As such a smart mouthed, intelligent, and beautiful woman that you are, I figured you would know that already." I sat quiet; he really had gone there with me. He was challenging me. He thought he had me all figured out.

"So Janelle, where's your husband?"

"He's in our room, handling work business."

"What does he do for a living?"

"Probably the same as you."

"You really think so?

"No. I was just saying. You guys both have secret careers."

"My career is not a secret; I just don't announce it to the world."

"Well, neither does my husband."

"Well take my card, contact me sometime. I need to leave now; I don't want to be late for work. Have a good day." He turned around and started walking to his car.

"I didn't say I was going to use it." He looked at me and smiled.

"You will." I got back into the car. A few seconds later Blake was coming out of the motel room. He was wearing a white t-shirt, a black ripped up pair of jeans, and his black Nike slides. He had on a gold watch that I've never seen before so it must have been new. Blake loved watches. If you named a watch, he had it. He never turned down an opportunity to buy a new one.

"Janelle, you ready?"

"Blake I've been ready. I was waiting for you."

"I love you."

"Look don't start." I looked out of the window, and I noticed that Saif was still sitting in his car. This time he was on the phone with someone, he didn't notice me staring this time, but I could tell he was succeeding at whatever his job was because that conversation seemed to be an interesting one and one that he had accomplished. Saif was so handsome; he made me think about not being with Blake at that moment since our relationship was no longer what it used to be. I wanted our relationship to work out, but actually being home, I wasn't sure if I could trust Blake. I didn't know if I could love him the same as a few months before. Blake was my lover, my rock, my

302

everything, but he had become nothing but someone I had a child with and even my son reminded me too much of him. I hardly had a relationship with him. Could I start over?

Chapter 29

The only clothing store in town was a Kmart and a sledding place across the street. The town was old; it had a few drug stores. It had one doctor's office, which was combined with a dentist and an urgent care. The hospital wasn't close by so if they needed care right away they went there. I didn't know how long we were going to stay, but I knew I needed a new phone, some clothes, and some hair products. My hair desperately needed some loving. It was extremely dry.

"Baby, who was that guy you were talking to?"

"Oh, um his name's Saif, I don't really know him; he had just introduced himself to me."

"He gave you his business card?"

"Oh yeah, he did, he was trying to hit on me."

"Janelle, so you like him? You find him attractive?"

"Why does it matter? Aren't we married?"

"So you still want to be my wife?"

"I didn't say all of that, but we are married."

"Janelle, I need to know if you are going to leave me. I need to know if you are done with me and if you're going to take my son away from me."

"Blake, where is this all coming from? If I leave, you know I am not that kind of person. I will never take your son away from you."

"I don't know what you will do Janelle; I know you are angry at me. I know I treated you wrong."

"Stop right there Blake. I will never take your son from you. Yes, I am angry! Yes, I am hurt, but remember you made me this way. I didn't choose to be this way because I once loved you. I once knew who you were. Now I am lost. I no longer know or feel the same way."

"And I am so sorry." I couldn't understand why Blake kept on telling me he was sorry because I knew that. I knew that he wanted to make things better, but he ruined it all. What more did he want from me? I needed him to stop apologizing. That wasn't going to make me forgive him or even fall in love with him again.

I turned to look at Blake, but he was already staring at me. He was pulling into the Kmart parking lot. He let out a sigh and leaned over and touched my face. I turned around to face him; he took his hand off my cheek and pushed his seat back all the way. I watched him while he kept staring at me. It felt like we were looking at each other for an eternity when Blake finally made a move. He leaned in closer and kissed me. The next thing I knew I was taking my shirt off. Blake was unbuttoning my bra, and his pants were no longer around his waist. We kissed each other passionately while he entered inside me. We hadn't made love in a long time. I was still mad at him. Yes, he was hitting it right, but Blake and I were nothing but two people making love in the front seat of my truck in the Kmart parking lot.

We finally went into the store, and we couldn't keep our hands off of each other. Just from lovemaking, we were not thinking about what had happened, and we were both enjoying each other's company. We laughed and shopped for a few outfits, underclothes, bathroom items, and the rest of the things we needed for our temporary stay. We didn't discuss when we were going to go back home and really handle life. I didn't ever tell him about Darryl, and I hadn't talked to Darryl since he came to the prison to confess his love for me. I wanted to call him and see what was up, but it didn't feel right at that moment. I needed to go home and deal with him. I didn't know if I wanted to stay with my husband. But then again, I wanted to leave him and start over. He did still hurt and betray me, but who else would take care of me like him.

"Janelle, hold on. Let me take this call real quick." Blake walked away from me, and I continued to walk around the store looking for anything else that we had needed. I didn't want to have to come back if we didn't have too. As I passed the baby clothes, I started thinking about Junior; I hadn't seen him since the last few pictures that Blake's sister had sent me. He was getting so big, and I was missing out on it. I bet he would be calling his aunt Mommy, and I knew she wouldn't correct him if I wasn't able to see him until he was older. I didn't know when I would be able to be with him again. I was out of jail, and some things were a lot different, but I needed my son. A lady was holding her son in her arms walking around laughing with him, talking to him, making sure his every needs were met, and I couldn't even see mine.

"Baby, I'm coming, hold on." Blake had called out from behind me jogging. I stopped and watched him jog over to me. He wasn't smiling; he looked like he had something to tell me.

"What do you have to tell me?"

"Baby nothing, give me a kiss I love you." I turned around and kept walking. While we were walking around the store, there was tension between us. I knew Blake was lying and he knew that I knew, but he wasn't going to ruin the mood unless I made him. He was aware that I would be upset, so he didn't bring it up until we got into the car.

"Nells, we should get away for a little bit, get out of this town?''

"Why?"

"Well, don't you want to see something different before we go home?"

"Nope, I like it out here, when you want to go home, we will go. Until then I want to stay right here."

"Look at me."

"No, just say you have to leave for work again. Just go and come back already. I don't want to hear your lies."

"I wasn't lying; you would get away, I just needed to work for a day."

"Blake you say a day, and a day turns into three. I know how your shit goes."

"Not this time baby; it's different."

"Same shit, different day. I know."

"I'm sorry."

"Stop saying you're sorry; I get it."

When we got back to the motel, Blake helped me with all of the bags. We put away what we could. Then I watched Blake pack his overnight bag. He was packing and watching my every move; I just sat on the bed reading one of the books I had purchased. He answered a few phone calls and then brought his bag out to the truck. He came back in and looked around to see if he was forgetting anything. I looked up from the book and waited for him to look at me. We looked each other in the eyes.

"Blake I love you, and I'm sorry. Be safe; please call me when you've made it."

"I love you too, Nells. Here's some money and my credit card if you need to get around and buy some more things. I'll be back in a day, and if I have to stay longer baby, I promise I will call you and make it up to you when I return."

"Alright, babe but if I don't answer, I'll probably be hanging out with my new friend from down the hall."

"Girl, you better not be having sex with him when I'm gone. I gave you the greatest and will always give you the greatest.'' Blake walked over and gave me a kiss. He walked out, and I watched him from the door. He drove off. I shut the door.

Chapter 30

"Hey, beautiful." I looked up from my book and looked up to see Saif walking from his car over to me. The blue jacket that he had on earlier was now on his arms, and his shirt was still unbuttoned. He was carrying a box and a few books in his hands.

"Hey Saif, how's your day going?"

"It's good now that I got to see you."

"Why do you keep doing this?"

"Because you are beautiful, you have been on my mind all day." Saif was looking around in the parking lot and into all of the rooms.

"What are you looking for?"

"Your husband, he's not here?''

"No, he's not. Why does that matter to you?"

"So what were you reading?"

"Oh um, just some poetry."

"Poetry huh, do you write?"

"No, I don't. I just enjoy reading it."

"Come follow me. I have to show you something."

"Follow you into your room. No thank you."

"Come on Janelle; I don't bite."

"Biting isn't what I am afraid of."

He smirked and started walking to his room. I picked up my book and walked behind him. He sat down the box he was holding and opened the door. He motioned me to go in before him. He bent down to pick up the box. Before I walked into the room, I looked behind to see if Blake was going to pull into the parking lot, but he didn't. I knew he wasn't coming back anytime soon because he was away for an emergency work meeting. He wanted me to go with him, but I wasn't in the mood. I didn't want to stay in a hotel with him while he worked. He was only going to be gone for one day, so I figured I would be fine. Seeing Saif wasn't making my night better because I knew that he was the same exact person as Blake. They both were handsome businessmen and knew exactly what to do and say to a woman. They both were going to be the death of me. Darryl on the other hand was the total opposite; he loved first. He was honest and was always himself; he had no game which was why we had great chemistry.

I was walking into the ring with this guy, which I had no clue as to who he was and what he had up his sleeve. The first thing I noticed was the pictures he had out on the night stand. He had this huge black blanket on the bed. I sat down on the bed and picked up the picture frame. The woman in the picture was beautiful. She had really dark hair and her skin was glowing; she looked extremely happy. The kids were the spitting image of him. He couldn't deny them even if he tried. As I placed the pictures back on the night stand, I watched Saif fumble through his drawers. He was taking out some clothes. I watched him grab a sweater and a pair of jeans. He walked into the bathroom still not saying a word. I watched him turn the water on to the shower; he came back into the room and picked up a fresh towel from the cabinet in the closet and walk back to the drawer to grab his body wash. He smiled and went back into the bathroom. I really couldn't figure this guy out; he was very secretive. There was something about him that I wanted to get to know. I wanted to know why he desired to have more than one wife when she was so beautiful and looked like she had love in her eyes in that picture. I wanted to know why he decided to talk to me and why he invited me into his room knowing that I am a married woman. So many questions were going through my mind, and I got up from his bed and left. I went into my room and lay down on the bed. I grabbed the remote on the table and began flipping through the channels; I landed on a cooking show and watched it until I drifted off to sleep.

After what seemed about three hours later. I woke up to someone knocking on my door. The person kept knocking until I got up and finally answered. Saif was standing there with four coffee cups from the deli, which I assumed to be the one down the street.

He was standing there with the biggest smile on his face.

"Hey, why'd you leave?"

"Because you were in the shower and I didn't want to stay."
One of my curls were hanging in my face, and he reached out and
pushed it behind my ear. This guy was acting as if we knew each
other and it was his place to touch my hair and try to be romantic.
He was a complete stranger. We knew nothing about each other, and
I was allowing him to feel like everything he did was okay.

"Well, can I come in? Do you drink coffee?"

"Sure, come in." I opened the door wide enough for him to
come in but not wide enough for anyone to see inside. He sat on the
bed right away, took his shoes off and took one of the cups out of the
cup holder and began drinking.

"Yes, get comfortable. Make yourself at home."

"You are very sarcastic aren't you?" I shot him a smile and
shut the door behind me. I walked over to the other side of the bed

and sat down. I was about to pick up the remote when he grabbed it and turned the TV off. He placed the remote on the nightstand next to him and grabbed the cup holder.

"Oh, no thank you. I don't drink coffee."

"Well then take a cup of tea. One of them has regular tea, and the other has green tea."

"I'll take the green tea. Thank you."

"No problem, I knew you would have taken the green tea. You look like a green tea kind of girl."

"What does a green tea kind of girl look like?"

"Well, you look like you love hard. You look like you are open to new adventures and new people. You don't look like you take shit from anyone. When we first met, you looked like you were passionate. Your eyes were glowing; they seemed filled with a little tension, but they still were glowing with some sort of passion."

"So that's your idea of a green tea girl? Okay, Saif."

317

"So Janelle tell me what you do for a living?"

"Well, I am a stay at home mother."

"Why, because of your husband?"

"Absolutely not…" I turned to the side trying not to let him see me crying. I quickly wiped the tears and continued to talk to him.

"My brother was murdered, and I stopped going to school. I took his death really hard and haven't been ready to go back yet."

"How long have you and your husband been married?"

"Five years. Five long years."

"What are you passionate about, Janelle?"

"Well, I love law; I love helping others. I am very passionate about the people I love."

"Would you love me?"

"Saif, I don't even know you."

"Okay, so I am Pakistani, Muslim of course, I have one wife and three kids, which you know. I am over here for work; I was born in the United States but moved to my country a few years ago to marry my wife. I would love to marry another woman someday and show her that my views aren't wrong and how I will love her as much as she loves me. I went to school to be a teacher but changed fields when my parents died.'' Saif put his coffee on the night stand, lay back on the bed, crossed his legs, and looked up at the ceiling.

"So why did you invite me to your room earlier and then hop in the shower and not say anything?"

"I was testing you. I wanted to see if you would join me; I wanted to see if you really loved your husband."

"Are you serious?

"Yes, if you would have joined me, I would have known what kind of person you were, but you didn't. You showed me something different."

"So since I let you into my room and my husband's not around, what does that say about me now?"

"It says you respect your marriage, but you want to see and know me. You're not as innocent as you say you are."

"You think you know me, huh?"

"I don't think I know you; I'm just trying to figure you out."

"Saif, why do you want to figure me out?"

"When I saw you the other day sitting in your car, I knew right then I needed to know who you were. Your curly hair, your awesome smile, your voice and even the slight curves your body has in those black jeans you wore. Everything about you was interesting."

"But I am married, and you are still trying. Why?"

"Because I don't give up easily."

"You are crazy. Do you know that?"

"No, I'm not. You don't find me attractive or interesting?"

"Well you are good looking, definitely not someone I would have picked up on in a crowd, but you do make me wonder who you really are. That's the only reason why I let you in."

"So Janelle, why don't you leave your husband?"

"It's not that easy if that was what I wanted." I turned around and lay on my stomach, took off my sweater and watched Saif turn on his side.

"So then what's stopping you?"

"It's not that easy."

"Just talk to me."

"You are not going to believe this but do you remember when I told you about how my brother was murdered. Well …" I didn't want to tell him about what had happened but I needed to talk to someone other than my husband. I needed someone to know how I felt and how hurt I still was.

"He was murdered by my husband." I was staring at him, waiting for him to respond or show any emotion, but he didn't. He just lay there and looked at me crying. I got up from the bed and walked into the bathroom. I sat down on the bathroom toilet and cried my eyes out. I was so overly upset that I was hyperventilating. I could see that Saif was still lying on the bed; he didn't move a muscle. I couldn't breathe so I got up from the toilet and walked around trying to stop crying. I pulled my hair out of the bun it was in and let it fall to my shoulders. The more I tried to calm myself down, the faster the tears came down, and the harder it was to breathe. The last thing I remember was everything going black. Then I felt myself falling to the floor. I was lying on top of Saif's body; I was literally on top of him. He was playing in my hair and had a wet rag on my head. My head was pounding, and Saif's heart was beating slow and steady. It was calm. His chest moved up and down while he rubbed my back. I tried to get up, but I was dizzy. I felt like I was going to pass out again.

"Janelle, please don't get up. Lie back down."

322

"No, please let me get up."

"No, I won't let you. You need to be comforted. Let me do that."

"You're not my husband." I tried to get up, but he grabbed my face and kissed me on the forehead.

"Lie down."

Chapter 31

"Can you help me kill my husband?" I got up from on top of Saif and looked him in the eyes. He looked at me with a smirk on his face.

"Are you serious?"

"I think so. I deserve better; I deserve to be happy. Right?"

"You do, but will that make you happy?"

"I don't know; it sounds like a good idea."

"Well, it could be but do you have a plan?"

"No. Do I need a plan?"

"Yes, you do, what are you going to kill him with? What are you going to do with the body? Will you leave it hear or dump it? You need to know these things."

"You can help me." Saif sat up on the bed and grabbed my hands. He was holding them tight.

"Janelle, I need you to understand what you are asking me."

"I know what I am asking you; I need your help. I have some cash and his credit card. I can't buy the gun with his credit card but I can with the cash he gave me earlier."

"So what do you need from me?"

"I need you to be here for me."

"Janelle, I don't usually do this. This is what I have hitmen for."

"Wait, you've had people killed before."

"If you want me to be honest with you, yes I have. When people play with my money, I have to do what I have to do." I got off the bed went over to the mirrors on the wall by the closet and tried to put my hair up in a bun, but I couldn't find a ponytail holder.

Saif jumped up behind me and grabbed me by my waist. He picked me up off of the ground and carried me back over to the bed.

"Saif, please put me down."

"Are you okay?"

"Yes I am; I didn't expect you to be the guy I thought you were."

"If you thought I was that guy, why did you let me in here?"

"Because, who could be worse than my husband?"

"You can trust me; I won't hurt you."

"Saif, that's what you say. I need your help. Are you going to help me or not?" Saif took a deep breath, put his hands on my legs, and squeezed them.

"Do you want sex?" Saif moved his hands up my thighs. He grabbed me by my waist and kissed me on my neck. He kissed me on my collar bones, pulled me closer, and lifted up my shirt. I couldn't believe he was trying to have sex with me at a time like that. I had just asked him to help me kill my husband, and all he wanted was to have sex.

"Saif?"

"Shh." He kissed me on the lips.

"No Saif, we can't do this."

"Why not?"

"Because I am saying no. Not like this, not right now." I couldn't tell if he was hearing me until he kissed me one last time and let my waist go. He got up off of me and lay next to me on the bed. He didn't say a word. He just looked up at the ceiling.

"I'm sorry, Saif."

"Don't be, I was overstepping my boundaries. I'm sorry. But if you want me to help you, you will definitely owe me big time."

"If sex is what you want, I got you." I smiled, and he leaned in and kissed me on the forehead.

"Janelle, can I ask you a question?"

"Sure what's up?"

"Did you have sex with your husband before he left? Is that why you won't let us have sex?

"We did, but that's not why."

"Okay. So I'll give you a gun when you are ready, it will be in my room. You just let me know when and I'll have it ready."

"Thank you so much. One last favor?"

"You need somewhere to stay?"

"Yes."

"You can stay with me." I got up, hopped on top of him, and kissed him while biting his lips. He grabbed my butt, squeezed it, and then let me go. He pushed me off and took his shirt off.

"What are you doing?"

"I'm going to take a cool shower. Stop teasing me."

It was 3:00 a.m. when Saif and I finished planning my attack on Blake. I was going to surprise him and get him into bed. I was going to handcuff him to the bed and get him to have sex. Once we were finished, I would bring up something from the murder and get him angry. I knew Blake wouldn't get angry, so I had to think of something else to bring up. Maybe I would bring up him cheating on me. I couldn't believe that I was going to murder my husband. Did he deserve to die? Did I really want to take his life? I wasn't sure if I would go through with it because deep down I was a little frightened. I was afraid of what Blake would think, how he felt, and if I wanted to love another man. I knew having Saif help me was a risk because I barely knew him, and I might have to have sex with him, or worse marry him. Saif seemed to be a great guy and our chemistry was good, but I also had great chemistry with two other guys. I mostly wanted to end Blake's life so that I could be at ease for what he did to me. If I was to leave him, he would hurt for a while; but if I took his life, he would be gone forever.

The next morning the door was opening, and at first I thought that it was Saif trying to get inside, but I heard Blake on the phone. He was talking pretty loud. The room was dark. I knew Saif and I didn't have sex, and he hadn't left anything there, but I shot up and tried to look around to see if I could see anything. I quickly lay back down and opened my eyes again when Blake came inside and the light from the sun came shining in.

"Did I wake you, baby. I'm sorry."

"No, you didn't. I was already awake."

"So why didn't you answer the door?"

"I didn't feel like getting up; my body hurts."

"Janelle, did you have sex with that man?"

"Blake, what are you talking about? No, I did not. I didn't even see him. And why are you home so early, I thought you had to spend the day there?"

"I did, but then the client's wife went into labor, and they were having serious problems, I canceled it and decided to come back early to be with you." Blake placed his bags down by the door and came walking over to the bed. He took his shirt off and climbed into bed pulling me in closer.

I stayed up waiting for him to fall asleep, but I didn't want to move, and he got back up. While I waited, I thought about the plan that I had set up. I didn't want to wait for late that night to make the move. Blake was happy, and it needed to stop. I needed him to realize that he wasn't going to get away with what he had done because in his mind he was probably laughing at me. I knew he loved me, but he was still my brother's killer. I looked over at the cable box, and it read 12:30 on the dot. I knew Saif would be sleeping because he said he was staying home. We were supposed to go over the plan a little more, but since Blake came home early, I needed to get it over with. I quietly climbed out my bed, put on my sneakers, and closed the door behind me. Blinded from the sun, I slowly walked passed the two rooms between us and then knocked on his door. The first time I knocked, he didn't answer. On the second knock, he opened the door. When I walked inside, he was naked standing behind the door. He it and grabbed a pair of his shorts that were lying on the chair. Saif was definitely working with something good and maybe sex with him wouldn't have been bad after all.

"Janelle, what are you doing here?''

"Blake came back; I waited for him to fall asleep and then I came over. This has to happen right now. Give me the gun?''

"Janelle, right now? Are you sure you still want to do this?''

"Yes, I do. I need too."

"Janelle, think about this."

"I thought about it since he got here, I am ready. I think."

"I think you need to sit down and really think about this again?''

"Saif, I thought about this all last night with you. You said it was a good idea. You were down last night when I said I would have sex with you." Saif stepped closer to me; he grabbed my arms and pushed me down on his bed.

332

"Janelle, it's not about the sex with you. Yes, I am sexually attracted to you, but I like you."

"So then help me."

"Janelle, I think this isn't a good idea, I think you should take a day to think."

"I did. I already thought about it. I thought about not doing it, I thought about our son. About how he was a daddy's boy and is only a year old. I thought about how much I would miss him, how much we use to love each other. I thought about how happy we were. I even thought about how easy it would be if I left him and moved on. But nothing made me happier than seeing him six feet under."

"If that's what you want, my guns in the closet on the top shelf."

"Thank you so much. I really do owe you." I ran over to the closet reached onto the shelf and felt around for the gun. Once I put my hands on it, my heart started beating fast. I had to calm down so

333

that I wouldn't have an asthma attack. As I grabbed the gun off the shelf, I turned towards Saif, and he was still standing by the door. He had his head down looking at the ground. I could tell he wanted to stop me, but he knew I didn't want to be stopped. I walked past him. He grabbed my hand, took the gun, and turned the silencer on.

"Thank you." I leaned in towards him and kissed him on the lips; he didn't kiss me back. He just let me go and opened the door. The sun was so bright it burned my eyes. The sound of Saifs closing the door was loud. He slammed it right behind me. I slowly walked passed the two doors between us and made my way to our room. The door was closed, and the inside was still dark. My heart was pounding out of my chest, and it was getting a little harder to breathe. I took a deep breath and walked inside. Blake was not in the bed; the bathroom door was closed so I aimed the gun right at the door. Blake had been in there for a while; I didn't hear any water running at first. I thought he had left and was playing a game with me. Finally, the bathroom door opened and he walked out. I had the gun aiming right at him. Blake was shocked; he was standing at the door watching me. His eyes were on the gun.

"Janelle, what is going on?"

"You should already know. Haven't you seen a gun before?"

"What are you doing?"

"Stop asking me questions. Shut up?" Blake was holding his hand up in the air. He was breathing hard.

"Blake tell me why you don't deserve to die.''

"Nells …"

"Do not call me Nells! Why don't you deserve to die?"

"I am your husband. I love you. Please."

"Did you think about me being your wife when you killed my brother? I don't think you did."

"I did Janelle; I swear I did."

"I don't believe you!"

"I swear I did."

"Stop lying!"

"Okay, I'm sorry please let's talk about this."

"Talk about what? We already talked about it; it's done. My brother is dead, and we both know how sorry you are. I get it."

"What about our son?"

"Don't bring Junior into this. You know they took him away from me, and I can never see him again. You did this! You bastard! You did this!" I was aiming the gun at Blake when someone busted through the door. It was Saif. He came in behind me and grabbed me by the arm. I was so confused as to why he would come in here and ruin the plan.

"Saif, get back. Don't touch me!" He moved his hand off of me and stepped to the side of the room. Blake was looking at him with rage in his eyes. Blake was not taking his eyes off of him. He was more concerned with Saif than me. I needed him to see my pain, my hurt and everything I felt. He needed to feel like I did.

"Blake are you ready to die?"

"Janelle, please you don't want to do this."

"Yes, Janelle listen to him; you need to think about this."

"SHUT UP!"

Keep up with me.

Contact info:

Website: www.shanikuabrown.com

Email: shanikuabinfo@gmail.com

Social Media:

Instagram: @authorsmb

Twitter: @authorsmb

Facebook: theauthorsmb